SURROUNDED BY Woods

USA TODAY BESTSELLING AUTHOR

MANDY HARBIN

Copyright © 2011, 2016, 2020 by Mandy Harbin

SURROUNDED BY WOODS
ISBN: 978-1-941467-50-3
ALL RIGHTS RESERVED

Cover Art by Letitia Hasser | RBA Designs

This book may not be reproduced or used in whole or in part by any existing means without written permission from Mandy Harbin, M.W. Muse, Penning Princess Publishing, or Mandolin Park, LLC.

This book is a work of fiction and any resemblance to persons, living or dead, or actual events is purely coincidental. The characters are products of the author's imagination and used fictitiously.

For more information, please join Mandy Harbin's Newsletter!

*To Mom, for taking the time to read my
stories and provide feedback I could
actually use, rather than just gushing over
how awesome I am.*

CHAPTER ONE

"You can't be serious, Bill." Mikaela Patterson pleaded with the senior partner of her law firm. "Mr. Woods is your client, and I'm already behind. I can't fly out to Texas for two weeks."

What she really wanted to do was crawl in a hole and die. She'd walked in on her fiancé and his secretary doing more than balancing financial statements in his office last month. She'd heard whispers of Joel being a creep, but she never understood. Just chalked it up to silly gossip. Until that moment of painful clarity. Amazing how seeing something like that opened one's eyes.

Mikaela called off the wedding, but she hadn't told anyone at her office yet.

She was a strong career woman and admitting what happened would make her look like a chump. Would she love to get away for two weeks? Absolutely. She would love nothing more than to spend two weeks in Cabo sandwiched between a cold margarita and a hot Miguel, licking her relationship wounds. Being thrown in the middle of her boss's work, a vacation did not make.

"I'm sorry, Mikaela. I have to be in Washington, and Mr. Woods is one of our biggest clients."

She groaned and crossed her arms, unable to hide her frustration.

"It'll be a cakewalk. Just go over the changes to his estate and draw up new papers."

"Why can't Sullivan or Smith handle it?"

"Sullivan is in the middle of that multi-million dollar lawsuit, and Smith is going with me."

She scrambled. "What about the newbie, Krista?"

"First of all, I'm not sending someone new to handle matters on one of our biggest clients. Second, she's single. Mr. Woods has specifically requested I send someone taken."

"I-I'm not married." Nope. She definitely was not that, and wouldn't be anytime soon.

"But you're engaged."

She wasn't that either. Not anymore, but she sure as hell wasn't ready to admit it. She needed to try another angle. "I'm a corporate attorney, Bill. I don't do estates."

"You do now. That is, if you want to make partner."

And there it was. She brought this firm in millions of dollars each quarter. That alone warranted a partnership, and Bill knew it. But he was also a cunning man who knew how to get what he wanted. Dangling the partnership in front of her hadn't been a thoughtless move. He was totally aware she wouldn't be able to ignore it. Well, he wasn't the only one who had this corporate game down. He might be her boss with many years on her, but she knew how to play, too.

And play it she would. She really had no other choice. "Fine. I'll fly out tomorrow."

"Now was that so hard?" Bill smirked.

"Take comfortable clothes. You'll be staying on his land with his family."

"Why?" she asked slowly, feeling her blood pressure spike.

"They own thousands of acres of timberland, and it'll be too cumbersome to get you in and out of the property each day. It's much easier this way."

Two weeks surrounded by woods. If they didn't have electricity and indoor plumbing, she would be staying in a hotel regardless of how long it took to get on and off the property. Why the hell hadn't she just booked that trip to Cabo like she wanted to last month?

Didn't matter now. She had a new client to work with.

After arranging her flight, she wrapped up what she could on her existing files and headed home to pack.

Comfy? She rolled her eyes as she tossed her things into her suitcases. She knew in her line of work she'd have to still dress smart if she wanted to be taken seriously. It was one of the few things she could control.

Apparently, it'd been the only thing within her grasp.

She'd overslept.

Her flight was delayed.

And even after she'd landed and thought she couldn't run into any more ridiculous problems, she'd tripped over her dang stilettos as she dragged her suitcases into the back of the truck she'd rented. She was off to a rocky start.

Bill had informed her that Mr. Woods would have her picked up at the airport, but something told her she didn't want to be stranded on his property with no escape route. She'd secure her own transportation, thank you very much. Assuming the terrain would be too rough for a car, she opted for the biggest truck the rental company had. It was enormous, but it should be able to get her in and out of the woods with ease.

After hours of traveling down the highway, she finally came to the small town that her navigation system refused to acknowledge. She found the turn off with the directions Bill had given to her before she left and felt relieved to know she wasn't really lost. No wonder Bill said she'd be staying on the property. The last hotel she passed was at least sixty miles back. With her next turn, she encountered a massive gate. She stared at it a minute, looking for some intercom to request entrance. Not seeing anything of the sort, she started to get out of the truck, but then the gate opened. Shrugging, she shut the door and drove through. At least the road was still paved. A lingering sign of civilization. She doubted it would continue to be that way for long.

At least she was here. Finally.

JOSH WATCHED the truck ease down the road and knew it contained the woman. Thomas had warned Josh and his brothers about her, about the fact that she'd be here to do some legal work instead of his regular attorney. That only meant one thing—she was taken. His father never allowed an untaken woman on the property because he knew it was too dangerous with four unmated sons. Josh being the eldest and most presumptuous of Thomas's sons.

Whether the woman was taken or not didn't really matter to Josh's libido, though. She was still a woman, and it'd been a while since he'd gotten laid. It was too dangerous for the Woods men to just pick up a woman, so they often went without. Since it was a rare occasion to have a woman on the property, everything about her presence was amplified. Without even seeing her, he could sense her. His feline senses first and foremost alerted him to the fact that she wore too much perfume. He'd have to cure her of that before she left; there was nothing sweeter than a woman's natural scent.

Trying to home in on her unique essence, he took another whiff and growled when he succeeded. His feral side fought to take charge, so he shook his head to clear it of the prime scent he inhaled, trying to forget the knowledge he'd just gained. She was ovulating, and he'd never smelled anything so potent, so intoxicating. He had to fight his instinct to stalk and mount her. He wanted nothing more in this moment than to claim her right now. Right fucking now! Feeling his control slipping, relief washed through him remembering she was taken. If she wasn't taken, he knew there'd be no way to stop himself from claiming her.

Since she was already taken, his humanity would prevail. It was a curse to his kind. A mountain lion shifter. His family was the only ones he knew of in the area, so they had to maintain their distance to ensure their protection and others' safety.

Needing to stay focused, Josh raced back toward his brothers, but one last thought nagged at him.

If she looked anything like she smelled, he was in trouble.

CHAPTER TWO

"Ah, Ms. Patterson. Please come in," Mr. Woods offered as Mikaela entered his office. Okay, so it wasn't Cabo, but the property was not as rustic as she'd feared. Although it was designed with the rustic feel, it was really anything but. The main residence was at least five thousand square feet with smaller cabins in the main clearing. The road was paved all the way to the house, which seemed to have every amenity available. "I have instructed Jeffery to take your bags to your room."

She walked forward, hand extended. "It's a pleasure to meet you, Mr. Woods."

He shook her hand. "Please call me Thomas."

"Then you must call me Mikaela." She smiled as she pulled her hand away.

"All right, Mikaela. I appreciate you coming here in Bill's place. I hope it wasn't too much of an inconvenience. I'm sure you're a busy woman."

"Oh, it was no trouble at all." No need to tell him about her little fit in Bill's office. She was a professional, so she really did know how to act like one when she needed to.

The door to his office swung open, and she turned to see who entered. *Who is that?* The man was hot! Not at all like the men she'd dated; she typically dated clean-cut professionals like her ex-CPA jackass of an ex-fiancé. But this man was huge and scruffy with tanned skin and brown hair. He looked like a lumberjack. *Lumberjack? Where'd that come from?* Must be because she was stuck in the middle of a forest. But he was definitely smoking hot. Just looking at him made her knees shake with possibilities. She realized she was still staring—well, ogling—so she jerked her attention back to Thomas.

"Is there a problem, Josh?"

Josh's eyes flashed to Mikaela and then

away before answering. But the moment his eyes landed on her, she could feel heat rushing through her. "Yeah, the tractor stalled out on the south ridge. I can't get Jack on the radio."

"Not good." Thomas turned toward Mikaela. "Mikaela, this is my eldest son, Joshua Woods. Josh, this is Bill's associate, Mikaela Patterson."

Josh stared at her, a smile playing at the corners of his lips. It took her half a second too long to whip into her attorney persona, but she kept her cringing internal at her lack of quick wit. She stepped over and shook his hand. "It's a pleasure to meet you."

His hands were calloused, and his eyes were as green as the forest that surrounded them. First she likened him to a lumberjack and then to the forest. This place was really messing with her head.

"Likewise, Mikaela. Can I call you Mikaela?" His thumb brushed the back of her hand as he shook it, not letting go.

"Um, of course." Don't stare at his chest!

She pulled her hand away and turned back to Thomas.

"I'm sorry, Mikaela, we'll have to cut

this meeting short, but I'm sure you want to get settled in any way. I need to go see what's going on with Jackson; he's one of my other sons. You can meet them all at dinner. Jeffery will come get you when it's ready. In the meantime, Josh will show you around." He faced his son. "And make sure you show her respect," he mumbled as he stepped out of the office.

———

JOSH COCKED his head to the side and nodded to his father as he stepped out, then turned his attention to the babe in the room. "This way." He took her arm without further words. If he spoke, he'd have to look at her. If he looked at her, he'd...he couldn't think about what he'd do. He could barely contain his thoughts.

God, this Mikaela sex kitten was the hottest thing he'd ever seen! Dark red hair and piercing blue eyes. It was like fire and water in one being. No way would that be possible in the wild. Fire and water couldn't coexist, but somehow, she'd harnessed those elements beautifully. He was definitely in trouble. Damn his luck for her being taken. She sure didn't respond like someone who was taken, though. He saw her eyeballing him in the office, and he could hear her heavy breathing right now as he took her to her room. He'd bet his left nut that she'd cream as soon as he slipped his hand up her shirt to play with those nice big tits. It took every bit of his humanity, his human nature, not to claim her here and now.

What was wrong with him? He'd been around other women and never once wanted to mate with them. Fuck them? Hell, yes. But those were carefully arranged encounters to protect everyone. As was this one. So why did Josh want to take and claim her? Why this one?

Rounding the corner, he tried to get his thoughts under control. He knew he couldn't take her, but his body demanded he do something.

Maybe as long as she was here and willing... *No!* He didn't even allow himself to finish the thought.

"Here's your room," Josh said as he opened the door and pulled her in.

Mikaela looked around and was noticeably shocked at how accommodating it appeared.

"Yes, you have a TV and everything," he teased.

She narrowed her eyes. "I see that. Internet?"

"Wireless."

"Cell phone reception?"

"That too."

"Bathroom?"

"Down the hall. Third door on the left."

She frowned, looking at the two doors in her room. He figured she was guessing what was hidden behind them, knowing she wouldn't like the idea of walking down the hall to shower. "Hmm, I thought there would be one in here."

Josh smiled. "Oh, there is. Through that door. But *my* room is down the hall, third door on the left." His eyebrows shot up, and he stepped toward her. God, her scent was maddening! Whatever control he held onto earlier was thrown eagerly out the window. He had to have her.

She stepped back, instantly realizing

his intent. "I have no need to know where *your* room is."

He continued his advance. "You might like mine better."

"How so?"

"I'd be in it."

That was an *oh shit* look if he'd ever seen one, and he flashed a grin.

"I'm here on official business, Josh. I'd appreciate it if you'd act like it."

"I won't do anything you don't want me to, kitten."

"It's Mikaela," she said sternly, standing her ground.

Josh stared. Damn, but she was a strong-willed woman. That made her even sexier. He wanted to bury his cock inside her, make her scream his name. "Fine, *Mikaela*. Just try not to fantasize about me too much. You're already blushing. With your fair skin and gorgeous red hair, I'd imagine that blush extends far below the neckline hidden in your designer shirt, all the way down to your pretty pussy."

She gasped. Just the reaction he wanted. Hell, he'd take any reaction from her.

His smile widened before he realized

he needed to get control of himself. He was a grown-ass man, not some horny teenager. Straightening his stance and wiping the grin off his face, he said, "Gym is on the first floor to the right of the stairs. Kitchen is to the left. Den's on the third floor. Copier, fax, and other business things you may need will be in the section of the house we just came from. Any questions?"

She crossed her arms and shook her head. He figured she couldn't speak even if she wanted to, though Josh wasn't sure if it was because of his flirting earlier or the fact that he wasn't flirting now.

"Good." He turned and left before she could find her voice.

And he realized he couldn't flee her fast enough. The woman was taken. Taken! He could not, would not try to take her. His reaction had to be because of his recent lack of female contact, but his body was acting like she was a potential mate. Impossible. And if he was acting like this, how would his brothers act? A possessive growl rumbled in his chest, and he bit it off. She was not his, and he couldn't act like she was. She was here on business, and he was going to respect that.

If he told himself that enough times, maybe he'd start to believe it, but even as he sought refuge in his room, he couldn't help but groan at this new predicament that was Mikaela Patterson. *What the hell am I going to do about her?*

CHAPTER THREE

WHAT THE HELL am I going to do about him? Mikaela thought as she finished unpacking her things to burn up time until dinner. No wonder Bill didn't want Krista coming here. If Josh was like this, there was no telling how his brothers would be. And what the hell was wrong with her? She just stood there like an idiot when he was coming on to her, trapped like some prey. She was an attorney, damn it! She knew how to argue and stand her ground. Sexy man or not, he'd not get the best of her. And she kept telling herself that all afternoon while she unpacked and fretted about the hot Woods son.

A knock sounded, making Mikaela jump. "Ms. Patterson?"

At least it wasn't Josh's voice. She got up and opened the door.

"I'm Jeffery. I am to escort you to dinner."

"Of course." She turned out the light and followed him down the hall.

When they rounded the corner, she heard rumblings coming from the dining room. She felt nervous and then silly for feeling nervous. She was here on business. It didn't matter that she found Josh incredibly hot. He was crude anyway, and she'd never find herself attracted to a man who acted like that if she wasn't stuck here.

Jeffery opened the door, and she stifled a gasp. She could give herself pep talks till she was blue in the face, but her body knew differently. Josh was quite possibly the prettiest man she'd ever seen.

Thomas and Josh stood talking to three other men, drinking what looked like scotch. All of them were well dressed, but the one who stood out the most was Josh, of course. Yum! He had on a forest green shirt to match his forest green eyes. Who cared about the forest, lumberjack association? It fit! His sleeves were rolled up to show his tanned, muscular arms. Was he that tall before? He stood taller than the rest of them, but just slightly.

Thomas walked toward her as she entered the room. "Mikaela, I'd like you to meet my other sons. This is Jackson, Robert, and Toby."

"Call me Jack," the one leaning passed Josh said as he took her hand.

"Rob," the one closest to her clarified, pulling her hand out of Jack's grasp.

"Just Toby," Toby said, making no attempt to touch her. "I have no nickname."

"And I'm Josh, in case you don't remember." He winked at her. How could she forget?

She laughed softly at Josh's comment, but couldn't maintain eye contact. She turned her gaze to each of his brothers and smiled. "It's a pleasure to meet you all. You have a beautiful home."

"Would you like a drink before dinner?" Thomas asked.

"Oh, no thanks. I haven't eaten much today, and I'm already a lightweight as it is."

Josh stepped closer to her as the others started for the table. She felt her heart racing but tried to act cool. "And what happens when you get liquored up?" he whispered.

"Normally my panties come off." Why did she just say that? "But that wouldn't happen now." Mikaela smiled to keep the words from being too harsh while she steadied her thoughts and berated herself for saying anything of the sort, only to realize she was flirting. As she thought about that, she smiled bigger; she didn't mind flirting a little. She liked it.

His eyes gleamed. She could tell he liked the idea of her being playful. "And why not? Do you have no faith in my abilities to charm them off you?" He brushed a strand of hair behind her ear, and she shuddered lightly, unable to control her body's reaction to him. But she was an attorney; she knew how to turn a situation around to suit her. She could still be flirtatious but maintain the upper hand.

"No. I'm not wearing any." She turned and walked to the table, but not before hearing his small gasp. *Good.*

She took the seat next to Toby. Josh took the seat next to Thomas who was sitting at the head of the table. It looked like the boys staged across from each other based on age. Josh and Jack sat across from each other with Rob sitting next to Josh and Toby next to Jack. With Mikaela sitting next to Toby, she was diagonal from Josh with a couple of people in the way. At least at meals she wouldn't have to worry about her reaction to him sitting right next to her.

Jeffery brought out the food, and everything smelled wonderful. She really was famished. She glanced up from the table, and her eyes immediately landed on Josh. He was staring at her, and she could feel the heat of his gaze from across the table. Apparently, where he sat wouldn't matter. It was going to be difficult for her to be in any room with him. She forced her gaze to the other men—all of them were looking down at their food—before turning her attention back to Josh. She didn't want to, but she could feel his eyes on her still. It was a reflex reaction to look again, she told herself. She raised her eyebrows in question, hoping for some kind of change in his stare. If she wasn't mistaken, he had a possessive, feral aura about him. And even with her staring back, he still didn't move, didn't change his posture. She cleared her throat and forced her attention to her dinner.

Once she started eating, she chanced a quick look at Josh. He was eating now too. Had he just been waiting for her to start eating before he started? She shrugged off that thought. The less she focused on him, the better off she'd be.

"So Mikaela, where did you attend law school?" Thomas asked from the head of the table.

She already felt uncomfortable under Josh's scrutiny, but this kind of attention was preferable. It would give her the opportunity to hide behind her attorney persona to woo her client and his family. It was a role she was much more comfortable portraying than that of a regular woman. "Loyola. I got a one seventy-five on the LSAT, went under scholarship, made law review, and clerked for the state supreme court. I usually focus on corporate law, but our firm handles all areas for our clients."

"That's good for us." Thomas chuckled.

"Yes, sir." She smiled.

They spent the rest of dinner asking about her job and her family, and every time she tried to put the attention on one of the guys at the table, they'd find a way to put it back on her. It was an exhausting exchange, not because she wasn't used to the attention, but because Josh refused to take his eyes off her. She felt like he was critiquing her every word, her every gesture, but she couldn't fathom why if he was just some guy coming on to her. By the time she finished her meal, she wanted to escape. She was too stubborn to admit that escaping everyone was the same thing as running from Josh, but she was smart enough to know that if she stuck around, she'd be running to him and not from him.

Mikaela knew she wasn't ready for that.

"If you'll excuse me, I'm ready to turn in." She stood, and every man at the table shot up in response.

"Breakfast is at six," Thomas said with a smile.

"Six?" Her voice cracked. As in a.m.? Who ate breakfast at the butt crack of dawn?

Thomas's smile became more pronounced. "Is that a problem?"

"No, no. Er, I just usually exercise before eating."

"You are welcome to wear your workout attire to breakfast. We only cleanup for dinner," Thomas reassured her.

There was that. "All right. I'll see you at breakfast."

Josh hurried around the table. "I'll see her to her room."

So much for escaping. He placed his hand on the small of her back without a response from her. She glanced at the other men at the table, and all of his brothers seemed to be glowering at him. Was he trying to stake his claim? For all they knew, she was unavailable.

He escorted her out of the dining room and up the stairs.

"Um, your brothers are nice," she said to make small talk as a reason to distract herself from his very warm, very gentle caress. She thought his gaze was hard to ignore. That was nothing compared to his touch.

He made a low noise that sounded like a disgusted groan, maybe even a growl. Apparently, that wasn't an appropriate topic for small talk, but Mikaela struggled to think of something else to say. His hand continued to rub soothing circles on her back, but with each circuit, he went lower and lower still.

Josh leaned toward her ear, his lips almost touching her skin. "You look lovely tonight. I'm sorry I didn't say it any sooner."

His breath made her shiver, and when his hand found her waist with a gentle squeeze, her heartbeat quickened.

"Thanks," she said a little too breathlessly. What was it about this man that got to her? She knew she shouldn't be flirting with him, but she couldn't stop herself from doing so at dinner. She enjoyed her responses as much as the ones she'd coaxed out of him. She surmised that a little flirting was harmless, but that still didn't explain her body's reaction to him.

He reached for her door, opened it, and turned on the light before shutting the door—with him inside her room. Just because she flirted a little and found him utterly delicious didn't mean she was going to jump into bed with him! Just last month she was engaged to another man. It surprised her that she hadn't really considered that fact earlier. The engagement was obviously a huge mistake, but until she came here, she hadn't really thought about moving on. Not that she still loved that jackass, but she just hadn't allowed herself to think about the future. Maybe there was more to Josh than she was willing to admit.

And Mikaela didn't want to admit anything right now, so she just glared at him for his presumptuous behavior.

"Goodnight," she said curtly. Regardless of what she was thinking, who'd he think was? God's gift to her? *If so, thank you, Jesus!* She felt she'd betrayed herself with that errant thought. Her brain and her body were definitely not in agreement. She was all over the place! But she was a smart woman who made a lot of money off her brain, so she forced her brain to prevail now.

He took a step toward her, and she stood her ground; she was *not* backing away from him like she had earlier.

"You're a strong woman. I like that. A lot." He suddenly wrapped his arms around her waist and yanked her against him.

She gasped and put her hands on his chest in a defensive maneuver, though now she could feel his erection through his thin slacks, which made her brain foggy. So much for her brain prevailing and her being a smart woman. She couldn't focus on anything but his touch. "What are you doing?" she breathed.

He bent his head and sniffed along her neck to her ear, making her tremble, and she knew Josh could feel it. "Taking you in." His hands slipped down to cup her ass, and he groaned. "You're not wearing any panties."

"I told you I wasn't." She wondered—again—why she'd let that little bit of info slip out earlier.

"I thought you were just saying that to make me hard." He rubbed himself against her, and it took everything she had not to return the favor. "I have been ever since you said that."

He nibbled on her ear, and she moaned. God, he felt so good. Why hadn't she found the willpower to push him away? This was nuts! He was her client's son for crying out loud.

Josh wrenched himself from her ear and crushed his lips to hers. She gasped, giving him the open access he sought, and what little willpower she mustered in the last moment crumbled. Tasting faintly of scotch, his tongue plundered, stroking her tongue like he was fucking her mouth. Heat shot between her legs, and her pussy flooded with her juices. He felt so good, so confident, so strong, she didn't want him to stop.

She slid her hands into his hair and forced him to deepen the kiss. Groaning in satisfaction, he gave her what she wanted while grinding his cock against her belly. They kissed so frantically, nipping and sucking tongues, lips, that she wasn't sure how she remained standing. Then he grabbed her hips and slowly gathered her dress up on both sides.

"Are you wet for me?" he asked as he shoved her dress up around her waist, holding it with one hand, and sliding his other hand to cup her. He nipped and kissed her neck while he stroked her nether lips. "Oh, God, you don't have any hair."

His finger delved in, stroking her lightly but ignoring her clit, knowing it'd drive her crazy.

"Josh," she breathed.

"Yes, kitten. You're wet. You're so fucking wet." He slid two fingers inside her pussy and covered her mouth with his to capture her squeal. He pumped his fingers in and out while he groaned into her mouth.

He moved his thumb over her clit lightly enough to pleasure her, but too light to throw her over the rapturous edge she dangled on. His hands. God, his hands were more skilled than any other that had touched her before.

She clawed at his hair, pulling his head away so she could catch her breath, and he immediately kissed and nipped at her ear. This was too much, too good, but too much. She was suspended, trapped, and wanted release, needed it harder, faster. "Oh, God, stop teasing me, please."

He chuckled seductively. "I like it when you beg, kitten. Tell me what you want."

Mikaela groaned and got wetter just from the idea of telling him anything like that. She'd never been vocal during any sexual encounter. Sure, she'd moan and verbally enjoy what she experienced, but she'd never said anything she wanted. But she found that she liked the idea very much. "Faster," she barely breathed.

He pulled his face away from the crook of her neck and smiled at her, his eyes filled with lust and white-hot need. Some part of him must've realized and really liked the fact that this was new territory for her, making her vulnerable, considering she was such a strong woman. "Like this?" He moved faster, but didn't increase the pressure. He watched her face as she enjoyed the feel of his fingers in her pussy and on her clit.

"Yeah." She groaned. "Harder."

He yanked her up against the length of him, still holding her dress in one skillful hand. He shoved his fingers in and out of her pussy harder, faster while he rubbed her clit with the same assault. "Come for me, kitten. I want to feel your pussy squeezing my fingers."

"Josh!" Oh, God, he felt incredible. She was almost there, just a few more moments of his deft touch and she would be flying over that precipice into nirvana. She knew this was wrong, but she couldn't bring herself to care right now. All that mattered was his touch. Nothing else did.

The knock on the door jolted her out of her abandon. Josh stopped his ministrations, and they both looked toward the door, air billowing out of their lungs.

"Mikaela, sorry to disturb. Is Josh with you?"

It was Thomas.

"Shit," Josh whispered. "Yeah, I'm still here, Dad."

"Can I see you out in the hall?" It was a question, but it sounded like an order.

Josh slid his fingers slowly out of her, her pussy clenching around them in protestation, and she whimpered. "Sorry," he whispered. "We'll have to pick this up later." He licked his fingers with relish and groaned before dashing to the bathroom and washing up.

He opened the door within ten seconds. He nodded to his father and glanced at Mikaela. "Goodnight."

"Goodnight," she said to him. "And goodnight, Thomas," she said a little louder with a clear voice devoid any of any guilt or other emotion she shouldn't be displaying right after his son left her room.

"Goodnight, Mikaela," he called from the hall as Josh closed the door.

Thomas didn't sound convinced. He knew what they were up to. She just knew it, and he was under the impression that she was an engaged woman. She'd have to come clean with him. Granted, he was still her client and may consider any activity with his son inappropriate, but at least he wouldn't think she was some slut who'd fool around on her fiancé. Regardless, what happened tonight with Josh had been a mistake. It was very hot, but very wrong. With him gone, the fog in her brain cleared. She was here to do a job, not screw the hot son. What happened tonight wouldn't happen again.

She'd make sure of it.

CHAPTER FOUR

"WHAT THE HELL ARE YOU DOING?" Thomas barked at Josh as they walked down the hall, heading outside. "She's taken."

"She doesn't act like she's taken. Besides, I didn't do anything." At least he didn't get to *finish* anything. He'd wanted to rip her dress off, throw her on the bed, and shove his cock in every hole she had. Somewhere in the back of his mind, he knew he shouldn't have been doing anything with her, but she was so damned responsive. There was just something about her, something inside him that wanted to give her whatever she wanted. He'd love nothing more than to feel her come. He'd had every intention of making her come many times before he was finished, before he thrust his cock inside her and sought his own release in that very tight pussy of hers.

"Don't give me that shit, Josh. I can smell her on you. It's underneath the soap you used to try and cover up where your hands were, but my senses are much stronger than you give me credit for."

"Look, Dad—"

"No, you look, Josh. It stops right now. Right fucking now! You know damn well how dangerous this is. If you get too close to her, make her second guess her status with her fiancé, it could push you over the edge, make you want to claim her."

He did want to claim her. He'd wanted to the moment he first smelled her. The man wanted to make love to her; the animal wanted to subjugate and claim. But he wasn't about to confess that to his father. "I'm a lot stronger than Eric was."

"Eric thought he was a lot stronger than he turned out to be too. And where is he now? Dead. Along with the mate he claimed against her will."

There was no reasoning with him because, deep down, Josh knew his father was right. Just because he knew he was right, though, didn't mean he wanted to face that fact, so he dropped it entirely and asked where his brothers were. He wanted to hunt, and hunting would help him forget all about what he wanted from Mikaela.

"They're already out. They got tired of waiting for you."

Josh started for the door. "You coming?"

"Yes. I could use some fresh air."

Thomas and Josh went out back and stripped before shifting into their feline forms. They both sniffed the air and ground before heading out.

Josh looked at his dad. *This way,* he said telepathically. It was the only power his feline family had that could be considered supernatural besides the obvious ability to shift.

I know. Quit underestimating my sense of smell.

Josh growled at his father's stubbornness and at his own for knowing his father was right. He didn't want his father to be right, though. He wanted to be strong enough to claim Mikaela *after* she agreed to it. But that was the kicker, the reason he knew his father was right. When his kind was around an untaken female, the feral side was too dominant to control. If the mating was not consensual, the female attacked afterward. It was a black widow effect. She'd kill her mate out of spite, to gain a sense of control after that control was taken away through a forced mating, but she wasn't truly in control herself. Because the mating was too new in that type of situation, the male protected itself by attacking back. Injuries were usually too great to overcome, resulting in the death of both lions.

Each of them wanted a mate for life, but in order to mate, they needed an untaken woman. But when an untaken woman was around, all logic disappeared and the need to mate drove all instincts. Forcing a mating satisfied the initial desire for a lifelong mate, but it drastically reduced the lifespan to mere hours at best. It was a vicious cycle. One that had to be carefully played to ensure a successful mating. Thomas had done it years ago with their mother, so Josh knew it was possible. He always knew he'd figure out a way to make it happen, but now with Mikaela in the picture, he wanted to make it happen without a threat to either of their lives. He couldn't explain how he knew, but he could already tell that she had the potential to mean the world to him one day.

What's up, brother? Jack asked as Josh rounded the corner and found his brothers.

Nothing. Find anything?

We have some turkey over the hill.

Josh was grateful Jack wasn't pushing his buttons like their father was. *Good. Let's go.*

They all raced over and made their kill, feasting on the wild turkey. Such a primitive instinct, to kill. Josh knew that the animal within understood its priorities: food, shelter, mate. And these priorities would be met at all cost. But the animal within was not the man without. As a man, Josh understood the delicate circumstances surrounding claiming a mate.

Understanding didn't make things any easier.

After eating their fill, their languid cat-like selves became too much to ignore. If they didn't get back, they'd end up sleeping in the woods. They trotted back to the house, shifted, and dressed before going their separate ways. Josh started to pass

Mikaela's door on the way to his room, but stopped, tracing his hand along the rustic wooden door, his thoughts in a snarl. If he wanted to ensure her safety, there was only one thing he could do. On a sigh, he turned away and headed to his room. After crawling into bed, he fought sleep, searching for any other answer than the one he knew was right. When he accepted the fact that he'd have to let her go before even having her, darkness finally found him.

———

MIKAELA SLID into her tight shorts, sports bra, and fitted tank top. She hadn't gotten much sleep last night. After Josh got called away, she tried to ignore her aching need, but she ended up taking matters into her own hands. Not nearly as good as it had been before, but she'd figured it would ease her pent up lust and help her sleep. She was wrong. She still tossed and turned until her alarm went off thirty minutes ago. Whenever she was awake, she thought about Josh. His hands belonged to a masseur, not to a man who looked like he could defend what was his and kill to protect with his bare hands. His touch was so soothing, yet passionate. Gentle, but commanding. Never had a man brought her that close to orgasm that quickly.

After getting dressed, she wavered on whether she should wear makeup. She wasn't one to dress up to exercise, and she'd be taking a shower right after. It seemed silly to wear it, but she almost did. Almost. She realized she wanted to wear it to look good for Josh, and that was a mistake. She didn't need to do anything to encourage him. Remembering her resolve from last night, she scrubbed her face clean and threw her hair in a ponytail before heading out the door, smelling of soap and deodorant.

When she walked into the dining room, all eyes were on her. She just knew they all knew she and Josh had gotten busy after dinner last night. She swallowed at the thought and felt a light blush color her cheeks when she met Josh's gaze. He smiled softly at her. She quickly looked away while she walked over to the table to join everyone.

"I didn't even know this hour existed."

She chuckled, sitting down and eyeing the coffee before her.

The men laughed with her, easing her discomfort a little.

She took a sip of her coffee, enjoying the aroma as both a means to wake up and to brace herself for whatever topic lay ahead. She assumed no one would broach an inappropriate subject like the titillating touch of the sexy man across from her, the one she couldn't force herself to look square in the eye, but she didn't really know these men. She had no idea if they'd take the high road or not. God, she hoped so.

"Can you meet me in my office at nine, Mikaela?" Thomas asked. "I need to give you the old estate papers and discuss the changes. Will that give you enough time for your morning routine?"

She looked up from her coffee long enough to answer. "Nine is fine."

"Are you all right?" he asked. "You look a little tired."

"That's because I am." She smiled, taking another sip and forcing her gaze away from her coffee. She didn't mind them thinking the only thing that bothered her was this wretched hour, but she didn't

want to take the chance on them specu-
lating other reasons.

Her eyes went to Josh of their own voli-
tion, but now that she actually looked at
him, she noticed he seemed distant, almost
cold. Maybe he realized the mistake that
was last night and wasn't going to push it.

She wasn't sure how she felt about that.

Toby leaned over toward her. "You
don't have to meet us for breakfast in the
mornings. We just like to get an early start
with the trees."

"Trees? What do you mean?" This, at
least, provided a distraction.

"Cutting and prepping them for sale
and planting new ones."

She couldn't contain her giggle, so she
put her coffee down before she spilled it all
over herself. "You mean you're
lumberjacks?"

Rob's eyes cut to her. "That's not a bad
thing."

She sobered immediately, realizing her
tone was offensive. "Oh, I know. It's just
that my only visual of a lumberjack doesn't
really mesh with the real thing." She
couldn't say that she'd thought of Josh as a
sexy lumberjack the first moment she saw

him. But the reality of it was that he was sexy, and apparently, he was a lumberjack. Her initial description wasn't as farfetched as she originally thought, so she'd found it funny. She was laughing at herself, not them.

Thankfully, they all seemed appeased by her response. While she looked at each of the men, her gaze landed on Josh again. He still seemed aloof. Clearing her throat and looking at Toby and Jack, she asked, "So what time do you all meet for lunch?"

"We don't," Jack replied. "We try to eat together if we can, but usually have better luck with breakfast and dinner. Everyone is pretty much on their own during lunch."

That was a relief. Mikaela didn't like the idea of stopping her work just to meet up for lunch, and if they ate breakfast at this ungodly hour, they'd probably want to eat lunch just when she'd get her workday started.

They all finished eating and began dispersing. Thomas headed to his office, and Josh's brothers gathered to leave, but they were not going without Josh. He rose and walked over to Mikaela, who was standing up and finishing the last of her coffee. The look in his eye went from clinical to heated within seconds of reaching her. Without saying anything, he leaned in as close as he possibly could without making contact and sniffed. A strangled groan escaped his lips.

"You smell heavenly, almost as good as you look," he whispered. "If you're avoiding wearing perfume and makeup as a deterrent for me, it's not going to work. Your natural beauty far outshines anything you could do to cover it up."

She pulled away from him, shoulders square. "I'm just ready to exercise. That's all. I didn't put any thought into how you'd take my appearance."

She was sure Josh noticed she tried a little too hard when she said that and stifled a curse at her lack of composure. "Lucky for me you didn't." He leaned in closer, and her body trembled with excitement. "This is how I'll be visualizing you when I stroke my cock in the shower after work. It's the third door on the left if you want to come watch. I might even let you play with my balls."

Just the thought of being alone with him in the shower caused heat to shoot to her pussy, flooding her, readying her for his penetration. How could she get so turned on so quickly by him?

His nostrils flared, and he sniffed her again, groaning louder this time. "You're a naughty little girl," he murmured.

No way could he tell she was turned on. No way!

Someone cleared his throat, and Josh jerked his attention away from Mikaela.

"You ready?" Jack asked.

Josh took a deep breath and nodded, his eyes changing back to that mask of indifference from earlier, but right before, she noticed a hint of regret. Then he left without another word to her.

Smooth, Mikaela. Real Smooth. So she couldn't control her body's reaction to him, but she sure as hell could control what she did about it. And even though Josh had talked dirty to her right before he left, she got the feeling that he, too, was trying to control his behavior around her. The question was, why?

She didn't know, and she didn't have time to dwell on it. She worked out, showered, and was at Thomas's office promptly at nine o'clock. She did her best not to think about Josh, and she didn't. Much. But at least she tried to put him out of her mind.

"Here're the trust and will that Bill prepared for me a few years ago," Thomas said as she sat down.

She took the papers and scanned over them. "What changes do you want to make?"

"Everywhere Eric Woods is mentioned, I want him removed."

Eric Woods? A disowned son? No one mentioned him before. It was her obligation to make sure Thomas understood the implications of leaving a child out of his estate. "Thomas, if Eric Woods is a child of yours, he could contest this will if he's left out completely. It'd be in your best interest to leave him something, even if it's just your love and affection. If we don't mention him at all—"

"He's deceased," Thomas said flatly.

"Ah. Well, when an heir dies before an inheritance, the law dictates how his portion is to be divvied up. If he has any children, his inheritance would filter through to them. If he doesn't have any heirs, then what he would have received would be redistributed among your remaining heirs. A codicil isn't really necessary unless you plan on making other changes."

"I appreciate your advice, Mikaela, but I'd feel better if Eric isn't mentioned anywhere in my estate. He was my youngest and didn't have a wife or any children."

"Well, it's your money, Thomas." She chuckled. "I'd be happy to charge you for the changes."

He laughed with her. "I'm sure you would, but I do appreciate you trying to save me the money. I'd just like to have it done."

"Not a problem." She began to stand up.

"One more thing, Mikaela."

Uh-oh. Was he going to chastise her for her behavior last night? If so, she had no idea how she was going to handle the situation. She took a steadying breath. "Yes, Thomas?"

"I'd like for you to look over my business forms as well. I know it wasn't part of this trip, but since your expertise is in corporate law, I'd like to take advantage of that to make sure everything's airtight."

She felt her muscles relax and didn't even realize how tense she had been, thinking he was going to mention Josh. "I can do that. Since you do not have many changes to your estate, I should have plenty of time to look over everything."

"Great."

Yes, it was. If she buried herself in work, then she'd have no other choice than to focus on that and not on one Josh Woods.

Hmm... Maybe that was Thomas's goal after all.

CHAPTER FIVE

MIKAELA SPENT the next several days with her nose in her work and her eyes off Josh. She opted out of getting up early for breakfast and spent her days barricaded in the spare office next to Thomas's. If she worked really hard, she could get through everything in another day or two and head back early.

On two occasions during the day, she ran into Josh in the kitchen—once when she went to grab some lunch and another when she was getting a drink. Both times, he smiled politely and found the quickest excuse to leave. If she wasn't trying to avoid him just as much as it seemed he was doing his damnedest to avoid her, she might've felt offended. He *had* had his fingers inside her pussy the other night, and that following morning, he hadn't minded elaborating on her being his jerking off material. Regardless of how she felt about his avoidance, she knew it was for the best.

But no matter how much she tried to avoid Josh during the day, there was no getting away from him at dinner. Thomas insisted she break for dinner, feeling guilty she was working so hard. She didn't have the heart to tell him that she'd much rather keep at her work than face the temptation that his son presented. So she went, but she didn't dress up. She worked in suits and stayed in them at dinner. It was a reminder to everyone what her role was here. She was their attorney. Not Josh's plaything.

"Are you ready to go down for dinner, Mikaela?" Thomas asked, peering around the door of her temporary office.

"Give me two seconds." She locked her laptop and followed him out.

Everyone else was already in the dining room when they arrived. She expected as much. They all liked to have a drink before dinner, but Thomas had been staying back and working up until dinner just like Mikaela. She wasn't sure if he felt the need to do that since she was or if there was some other reason, but she was grateful that she didn't have to walk into the room alone. When she walked in with Thomas, Josh didn't show her any more attention than the other guys, just like the previous nights. She didn't know for sure, but she figured it helped Josh maintain his objectivity when Mikaela entered with Thomas. She knew that Josh's father could see his reaction if he showed any interest toward her, but she didn't care what the reason was. She was just glad he was backing off.

Or was she?

Even though she tried, she still couldn't shake the deep-rooted feelings that were building for Josh. It made no sense. She hardly knew him, but there was just something about him that called to her. Although she was doing her best to get finished with work early, there was a part of her that dreaded the idea of leaving here.

And it wasn't because she enjoyed being stuck in the woods.

"Would you like a drink?" Rob asked her as he handed his father a glass of scotch.

"Sure." Might as well. She'd been

working for days and felt like she could use one. Maybe it'd help take the edge off this thing she felt toward Josh. If not, maybe it'd just help her get through another evening and help her sleep.

"What would you like?" Josh asked as he stepped toward her. Even though he asked gently, his attention still startled her. It was the first time he'd singled her out since breakfast that first morning. As he approached, all she could do was ogle at the dusting of hair on his forearms, and as he got closer, she could smell his clean, masculine scent that contained a rustic, woodsy essence. He wasn't even touching her, and she was already mesmerized.

She looked up, but had to blink to focus on his face. "What do you have?"

"Practically everything." He smiled softly at her, and she couldn't help but smile back. He seemed so warm and inviting, not the cocky guy he had been originally, though if she were really being honest, she'd found that side of him attractive too. But more surprising, he was not being the cool, indifferent guy of late.

Stunned, she couldn't form a complete sentence. "Wine?"

"Red or white?"

"Red."

"Cabernet or merlot?"

Clearing her throat, she said, "Merlot would be great."

Josh turned and walked out of the room while everyone took seats around the table. He walked back with a bottle of wine, a corkscrew, and a glass. He stepped over to her at the table and set everything down before opening the wine and pouring her a glass. Because of how he was standing in relation to his family members, Mikaela was able to stare at him without everyone else noticing. It wasn't his handsome face or masculine chest she stared at. No, it was those wonderful hands. Hands that soothed her, hands that tortured her, for those hands did not get to pleasure her for long. Pleasure sampled then denied was nothing but torture because Mikaela knew what they were capable of.

Once Josh finished pouring her wine, he walked over to his seat without another word. She took a sip and glanced at him. He was staring at her, not that that was un-usual. Even over the last few days, he still stared at her and waited for her to start eating before he did, and she always looked at him before she'd start eating. It had been their only sense of connection during their time of avoidance, and some part of her was grateful that they at least had this. If not, she probably would've caved during one of their kitchen encounters by ripping off his pants and sucking his cock into her wanton mouth before he realized what was happening.

Knowing that Josh was still watching her, waiting for her to start eating, she decided she could take a step like he had by offering her the wine. She looked up and held his gaze, lifting her glass. "Thanks, this is really good."

He cocked his head to the side and smiled, seeming both genuinely surprised and pleased that she addressed him personally in front of everyone. "You're welcome."

Then his eyes seemed to dim before her very eyes, and he looked down at his plate. He still waited for her to eat before he dug in, but he didn't watch her.

So much for him not avoiding her anymore.

He was right, though, and she knew it. Getting involved with Josh would only lead to disaster. Mikaela just didn't understand what his reason was for avoiding her. Was it just because she was here on business and he was trying to respect that now? Or worse... Was he not really attracted to her? Oh, God, was she just a convenient lay that he realized wasn't worth the hassle? She'd hoped the wine tonight would help ease her, but what she really needed was a break. She had to get away from the temptation Josh presented, especially if that temptation was one-sided. She was immediately grateful that she never clarified about her broken engagement. No need to let that cat out of the bag now. It'd just raise questions as to why she kept quiet, and worst-case scenario, the knowledge that she'd essentially lied would probably fuel Josh's reasoning for leaving her alone, assuming he was even interested in her. Hating the idea that she could've misread his attraction, she suddenly felt trapped in the middle of nowhere. She had to get away from here.

Tonight.

———

THIS WAS MADNESS! She sat across the table from Josh, and he could feel her heat from where he sat. It was bad enough that he could smell her. Hell, he could smell her everywhere in this house. He'd spent his days working as far away from the house as he could and his nights running in his feline form just to try to get away from her. He didn't understand why she called to him, why he wanted her, why he needed her. She was becoming the center of his world, and he hadn't even fucked her. When he shut his eyes, he could still feel her pussy on his fingers, still smell her juices on his skin, still taste her on his tongue. She consumed him, and he hated it! Hated it because he couldn't do a damn thing about it. He tried his best to honor his father's wishes and not pursue her because he knew his father was right and he wanted to keep her safe. But he didn't have to like the fact that he was torturing himself by denying what his body and soul craved, especially when he felt she was the only woman who could fulfill his innermost desires.

Get a grip, Josh, Thomas warned. They usually saved this type of communication for when they were in their feline forms. It was a convenience, but it wasn't private. Everyone with the ability to communicate that way heard it as if the words were spoken aloud.

I'm doing what you asked, Dad. I've barely said anything to her in days.

You're not the only one who finds her attractive, Josh, Jack said. *I'd like nothing more than to claim her myself. This is difficult for all of us.*

Stay away from her! His eyes shot to Jack.

Back off, Josh. Jack's right. The only man in his room who doesn't want to bed her is Dad. Hell, even Toby can't stop staring at her, and she's much older than he is. Rob chuckled, and Mikaela's eyes shot over to him.

"Something funny?" she asked with a crooked smile.

All of them men looked at Rob. "Er, yeah. I just remembered something from a TV show I saw last night." He shrugged and took another bite of his dinner.

Smooth move, idiot, Josh griped, taking a swig of his drink.

Enough. No more mental communica-

tion with Mikaela in the room. She's a smart woman, and I don't want her to get suspicious.

Josh wanted to remind his father that he was the one who started it, but he realized that'd be a little too petty. Looking at his plate of food, he continued to eat his gourmet dinner, which tasted of wood chips. Nothing tasted right or smelled right with Mikaela around because all his senses focused on her whenever possible. Not that he minded. What was one more torture? He'd rather see and smell her from across the room and remember her taste than to not have her around at all. That wouldn't be torture because that notion was inconceivable.

As Josh pushed his plate away in dismay, Mikaela stood, and his eyes shot to her, all the guys fumbling to stand since gentlemen always stood when a lady stood.

"If you will excuse me, I'm going to step out for a while. I have some errands to run." She put her napkin on her plate and started to turn.

What the...? "Where are you going?" Josh blurted out. He couldn't stop himself from asking even if he wanted to.

She turned to face him, and he had to work hard at keeping his gaze indifferent.

She shrugged. "Out."

Out? What the hell did that mean?

As she started to leave, Josh darted around the table and clutched her arm. "Where?" he asked, staring down at her, stepping even closer into her personal space.

"I don't believe that's any of your business. But don't worry, I'm a big girl, Josh." She pulled her arm free and started for the door.

"Dad?" Josh whispered, and he knew he had a frantic sound in his voice. He didn't care. He needed help keeping her here. What if something happened to her? What if she got lost and couldn't find her way back? What if she got into an accident? Oh, God, he couldn't stop his mind from spinning with all the bad scenarios.

Thomas cleared his throat. "Mikaela, perhaps I could join you? You do not know your way around."

She turned around and looked at Thomas, refusing to meet Josh's gaze, which was good because he was panicked as hell. He didn't want his dad going with her either, but if she insisted on leaving, at least Thomas could watch out for her. Josh had no idea where she intended to go, and if there were going to be any untaken women around, that meant he couldn't insist on going with her, though he had to fight to remind himself of that.

"That's awfully kind of you, but it's unnecessary. I'm not sure how long I'll be gone."

Mikaela turned to leave.

Josh growled.

He knew he'd catch hell for letting his animal loose, but he didn't care. He did *not* want her leaving!

She stopped, clearly hearing his warning, straightened her back, and strode purposefully out the door without looking back.

"I'm following her," Josh said as he tried to leave the dining room. Regardless of the risk he faced running into untaken women, Mikaela was not going outside the property alone.

Thomas rushed around and stopped him, reminding him that Mikaela was here on business and could come and go as she pleased. She only stayed on the property as a convenience and was not Josh's personal toy. As he considered defying his father, his brothers moved around him. They knew he couldn't leave, and he knew he couldn't take all of them in an effort to escape.

Defeated, he spent the next several hours pacing the dining room, the den, his bedroom, and any other place his worried feet took him. By now, it was damn near midnight, so everyone else went to bed, but he just couldn't. Not until he knew she was safely home.

Home.

This wasn't her home, but he wanted it to be. More than anything. He knew he shouldn't think like that, and he'd been trying his best to keep his thoughts clear of any future with her, but right now, with her gone, he couldn't help but long for what wasn't his. When his soles were eating up the grass beside the driveway, he heard her truck finally making its way through the estate. Relief washed through him that she was safe, quickly returning to irritation.

He watched her park and get out. He wanted to march right up to her and ask her where the hell had she been...or march right up to her, fling her back up against the truck, and kiss her until neither one of them could breathe.

He could do neither.

Mikaela's eyes shot to Josh briefly, but it was long enough for him to notice that the irritation was mutual. She turned away from him and walked into the house. Without a word, he followed her in, staying two steps behind her.

She smelled like a parade of male and female cologne and reeked of cigarette smoke, which meant she'd been at a bar. He bit his lips so hard to keep from growling at her that his mouth bled. He paused beside her bedroom door while she opened it, staring at her back. She walked in and slammed it shut, and he walked to his own room.

Fighting the urge to shift and sleep right outside her door.

CHAPTER SIX

Mikaela stomped around her room, ripping off her suit, and hastily donning her pj's while her anger fumed. The nerve of that man! First, Josh acted like he was totally interested in her, then he abruptly changed his tune. Now, he was acting like some jealous lover. She yanked the brush through her snarled hair and realized she was too pissed to go to sleep. She wanted answers, and she was getting them. Right now!

Storming down the hallway, Mikaela didn't even knock when she reached the third door on the left. She gripped the cold knob and pushed it in, slamming the door shut behind her.

Josh's head snapped up when she

walked in. He was unbuttoning his shirt and had most of the buttons unfastened. His lightly furred chest stood proud, and Mikaela's fury briefly halted by the beauty of that man.

Briefly.

Stiffening her back and throwing her hands on her hips, she glared at him. "What the fuck's your problem?" she yelled.

His hands dropped from his shirt and balled at his sides. She saw his jaw ticking while he glared back, speechless.

Stewing over the fact that he refused to answer, she took two steps toward him while she tried to calm her tone. She could be mad, but she didn't want to just give him the upper hand by screaming a litany of questions. "What's the matter? Cat got your tongue?" she asked, barely controlling the volume of her voice.

His hands relaxed, and he chuckled without humor. It almost seemed as if he was laughing at some ironic, unfortunate inside joke. "Yeah," he finally said, returning to his task of unbuttoning his shirt.

Was he dismissing her? Why, that egotistical son of a bitch! "So you come on to me, ignore me, then act possessive? Why? If you're not interested in me—"

"Not interested?" He advanced on her, stopping inches from her. His eyes were green fire, heated from the depths of his soul. But he quickly shut his eyes, shook his head, and cleared his throat. When he opened his eyes again, they were back to that cool, green color, displaying that forced lack of interest.

"Right," she mumbled, turning for the door. Who was she kidding? If he didn't want to fess up to his actions, she couldn't make him, and if he wasn't interested in her, then standing here raving on about him only made her look that much more pathetic. The last time she felt like that was when she'd walked in on Joel and his secretary. Not a feeling she enjoyed.

As she whirled, she noticed his eyes lit on her breasts. Only then did she realize how revealing her pajamas were. The pants clung to her like a second skin, and the camisole top had sheer lace covering threadbare satin at her breasts. Not only were her nipples hard, he could make out the shape and shade of them. Knowing he peeked, whether he wanted to or not, only fed her irritation. He was a man. It was her experience that men looked at a nice pair of tits whenever the opportunity presented itself. It didn't mean anything. She stomped to the door and yanked it open. "Goodnight, asshole," she said as she slammed the door shut.

Once in the hallway, she heard a blood-curdling roar from his bedroom that made the hair on her neck stand. She'd heard him growl at her when she left after dinner and wondered how he managed to sound like that, but this roar sounded animalistic. No way could a man make that sound. A feeling of foreboding prickled her, so she quickly went back to her room.

As she climbed into bed, she couldn't help but think of Josh. Who was he really? What was his deal? And why was she so attracted to him? She allowed her mind to wander, her imagination getting the best of her at times, until sleep found her.

When she awoke, she was no closer to any answers, so she did the only thing she could think of. She renewed her purpose. Rather than avoid Josh, she would treat him like he was one of the others. Unexplained feelings or not, whatever had happened between the two of them would be forced behind her.

————

JOSH SHOWERED and headed to breakfast, but his movements felt mechanical. After Mikaela stormed out of his room last night, he spent the next couple of hours vacillating between anger for both her actions and her assumption that he wasn't interested in her to relief that if she'd drawn that conclusion, then she wouldn't pursue him. But as soon as he'd think about that, he'd remember she hadn't pursued him at all. He was the one pursuing her, and she was the one ignoring him. Okay, he was ignoring her too, but he didn't have any choice. He would not gamble with her life.

Not interested? If only that were the case. He'd never been more interested in another woman, or even another person for that matter.

Walking into the dining room, Josh braced himself for the lecture he knew he deserved. He'd acted possessive of Mikaela last night, and when she came into his room and called him on his actions, he'd roared after she stormed out. He knew that it was loud enough to wake his father and brothers, but they hadn't come to his aid. They knew what kind of sound he was making.

Pain.

Josh felt so bereft. He'd upset her, and he couldn't explain why. Sure, he was angry with her for leaving, but even most of that anger was directed internally. But knowing he upset her made him feel like he let her down. He was so shocked to see her walk into his room that, just for a moment, he forgot about his lot in life. He was a man who wanted the woman before him. And God, she was beautiful. Even if she was royally pissed at him. He now felt like she didn't even trust him, and no matter his reasoning for avoiding her—or trying to, at least—he didn't want to earn her distrust. If only he could explain to her about his feral side. The feline within felt like talk was overrated, but if it brought it one step closer to claiming Mikaela Patterson, it was all for it.

Thomas wasted no time letting Josh have it when he joined them. He listened and listened, and whenever his father paused from his berating long enough to inhale for another round of bitching, Josh used those moments to agree with Thomas. But he knew his father could go on and on, so he mainly sat there, listening to his dad's tirade while his brothers waited for Jeffery to bring in breakfast. Josh knew his father was right. He was just too tired and too lost to argue, so he acquiesced in an effort to minimize the damage. But while he verbally agreed to his father's take, Josh couldn't help but feel it wasn't fair that he couldn't just claim her and live happily ever after. What was most upsetting was that he wanted her to want that, too, but he knew that that would never happen.

Once Jeffery brought the food in, Josh got a much-needed respite. All the men filled their plates and began eating. Thankfully, the topic of conversation transitioned to work, affording his brothers an opportunity to join in.

While discussing the pine harvest and paper company mergers, the main door to the dining room opened. Josh looked up, his heart racing before he even saw Mikaela walk in. And he knew it was her. Not only was everyone else already in the dining room, but her luscious scent also assaulted him as soon as the door opened.

I thought she wasn't a morning person, Jack mentally said, but Josh didn't look at him. His eyes were locked on the door, waiting to see her. Just one quick look was all he was going to allow because if his eyes lingered, he wouldn't be able to stop himself from staring. But when he saw her, his head snapped down faster than he anticipated, his heart crashing in his chest. He expected her to be in her workout clothes, but she was in a robe! It looked like she had on the same pajamas as last night. When she had been in his room. God, he wished last night had turned out differently. Rather than fighting with her, he should've taken off her clothes and carried her to his bed. Knowing if he had to do it over again he still wouldn't allow himself to give in to his desire didn't help this little fantasy he had going on. He needed to not think about what was under that robe.

Josh heard her greet everyone as she sat down. He lifted his head to reciprocate the greeting, but didn't meet her eyes. When he looked back at his plate, he realized he still had his fork in his hand. His lion self chastised him, and he dropped his fork, it clinking loudly as it hit the plate. The reaction was purely an animal instinct, even though in the wild both male and female lions hunted on their own. But since he was a shifter, his animal demanded its female to eat first. He understood this characteristic from watching his parents; his mother typically did the hunting and brought the kill to his father. Since she'd make the kill, she'd eat first. So from their first dinner, Josh couldn't bring himself to eat before Mikaela. His lion wanted to claim her as his mate, and Josh knew that he couldn't. He felt like acknowledging her status at mealtime was a pitiful compromise, but it was the best he could do. Hopefully, she'd never ask why Josh did that. Once she picked up her fork and started eating, Josh retrieved his fork and continued.

"Did you find your way around okay last night, Mikaela?" Thomas asked.

She cleared her throat and nodded. "Sure did. And Josh was kind enough to stay up to make sure I made it back." What? Josh's eyes flashed to her, and she looked at him. "Thanks. I don't think I said that last night. I'd had a couple of drinks."

She shrugged with a giggle as she looked back at her plate.

What was going on? She was acting like last night didn't happen. She might've had a buzz, maybe, but she wasn't drunk enough to forget. "It was no big deal," Josh responded just as casually, taking another bite.

"I was thinking I could observe you all today," she said, looking at everyone. "You know, take a tour of the estate, see the type of work you do, the equipment you use. It'd give me a better understanding of your industry in case there are other legal matters I need to consider before leaving." Another bite.

"I think that's an excellent idea, Mikaela," Thomas said. "I need Josh to help me with some things, so Jack can show you around."

You better keep your fucking hands off her, Jack! Josh warned.

Don't worry, big brother. I wouldn't do anything you wouldn't do.

"Great. That is, unless you want to make it a group effort and let everyone show me the ropes? Well, except for you and Josh since you'll be busy." She looked at Josh with the same casual expression she used when she looked at Thomas.

"Er, sure. The rest of the guys can help."

Hot damn!

I'm not fucking playing, Rob. And before you squeal with excitement, the warning includes you too, Toby. Not a fucking finger—or paw—on her!

"Unless I'll be interrupting your work by having everyone show me around. I don't want to cause problems."

"It won't be a problem, Mikaela. In fact, it'd probably be more informative if we all join you. Josh and I can meet up after your tour."

Josh hoped his sigh of relief wasn't too noticeable. He didn't want one brother alone with her, much less all of them. He knew his father well enough to know he didn't need to meet with Josh about anything. But his little plan to keep him away from her backfired when she suggested the tour be a group effort. No matter how much his dad hated Josh's reaction to Mikaela, he was smart enough not to trust the rest of his sons alone with her either. At least now he could keep an eye on them and her.

After Mikaela dressed, the tour commenced. They spent three hours going over the grounds on ATVs, showing her the types of trees they planted and what each one was used for. They even gave a few demonstrations on how the trees were planted and cut with the heavy equipment. Mikaela asked all kinds of questions and genuinely seemed interested in what she was learning. She talked to everyone equally, including Josh. Toby even cracked a few lumberjack jokes, and Josh thought Mikaela found them funnier than they were. Maybe he'd just heard them all before. But hearing her laugh was like listening to a musical masterpiece. He'd felt the urge to keep saying funny things just to hear her laugh again.

"Is that a paw print?" Mikaela asked, squatting down to examine the dirt road they were on.

The guys kneeled down beside her and stared. Every one of them knew exactly what it was. They just didn't know which one of them put it there.

"Looks like it," Thomas said.

"What do you think it's from?"

"Looks like a cat to me," Toby said, chuckling.

Mikaela stood while Josh glared at Toby. What was he thinking acting like that?

"Cat? Seems awfully big for a little kitty cat." She smiled at Toby, probably wanting him to elaborate.

"I didn't mean that kind of cat." Toby smiled back at her, and Josh wanted to growl at him. Toby was flirting!

"Well, what did you mean?"

What, now Mikaela was flirting with Toby? Oh, this had to stop. "He meant mountain lions," Josh clarified.

Mikaela looked at Josh, eyebrows raised. "You mean cougars."

"Yeah, same thing." He shrugged.

"I thought they were west of here. Have you actually seen them on this property?" She seemed a little scared by that idea.

"Yeah, we've all seen them. It's okay, though, they won't hurt you."

"H-how many have you actually seen. At once, I mean?" she asked, stepping closer to Josh as if seeking protection. He really liked that.

"Um, I don't know. Four. Five. I guess." Josh couldn't help reaching out and stroking her arm to comfort her. He liked that her instinct was to draw nearer to him, but he didn't like the fact that she was scared.

"I thought cougars, mountain lions, whatever... I thought they were solitary animals. Only seeking out other cats when mating. Why would there be a group of them running around?"

She was way too observant and asking way too many questions. Josh didn't want to encourage her, so he tried his best to bring the subject to a close. "Don't know. Guess you'll have to ask them why." He smiled and started for one of the ATVs. His brothers followed.

Once Mikaela left, Josh and his brothers got to work, but his mind just wasn't on his tasks. He kept picturing Mikaela in her tight jeans and formfitting sweater. When she'd bent over, he watched how her jeans hugged around her firm, round ass. When she'd reached for a limb while studying a tree, he watched how her sweater crawled up, exposing her soft, light skin. Throughout the day and up until dinner, he kept his thoughts on her. As soon as he showered, he practically ran to the dining room just so he could see her that much sooner. He knew getting there faster wouldn't make her get there any quicker, but he just couldn't think logically.

After getting his scotch, Josh continued to think about the beautiful redhead staying here. After days and days of avoiding her and then fighting with her last night, today had been wonderful. She was so relaxed and eager to learn about his business that he felt a sense of pride. That wasn't uncommon, for he loved his work, but since Mikaela arrived, Josh's emotions had been all over the place. No matter how much he fought his feelings for her, and no matter how much he'd continue to do so, he couldn't deny the fact that he felt connected to her, and with each passing moment, that bond grew stronger.

When she walked into the room, his eyes lit up, betraying him. He didn't want to continue acting distant, but he didn't want to show how much he really liked her. He wouldn't even allow himself to explore the depths of his feelings for her for fear of what he'd discover.

Once she was seated, though, she'd been quiet for too long. He had to hear her voice.

"Would you like some wine, Mikaela?"

"Sure, thanks, Josh." That smile. He couldn't help but smile back.

After getting her wine and sitting down, Josh had the hardest time wiping the grin off his face. Being around her just felt too nice.

"So, Mikaela, when do you plan on getting married?" Thomas asked.

What? Why the hell would his dad ask that? Josh's smile evaporated on the breath he inhaled, bracing himself for her response. When he glanced at her, she was staring at Thomas with wide eyes. The question had obviously caught her by surprise, and Josh didn't understand why.

"I haven't decided."

That answer seemed calculated. He wondered if all her answers about her betrothed would be just as careful. One way to find out. "And what does your fiancé do?" Josh blurted out.

CHAPTER SEVEN

Oh, shit. Mikaela's eyes shot to Josh. First Thomas and now Josh. It was easier crafting half-truths for Thomas. "Joel is a CPA." That wasn't a lie, though. Joel was a CPA. He just wasn't her fiancé anymore. Mikaela hid her smile from her very lawyer-type response.

Josh grunted and took another bite.

"He's a very lucky man," Thomas offered.

"Yes, he is." Lucky she didn't castrate him, though his luck could still run out. And thinking of luck, why did hers have to run out now? Today had been really wonderful. All the guys had been helpful, funny, talkative. Even with all of them around, she still couldn't keep her eyes off

Josh, so when he easily jumped into the conversations or started new ones, her insides melted. Such a great day. She hoped it wouldn't have to end on a topic she wanted to avoid.

"Why don't you wear an engagement ring?" Rob asked.

What was with the inquisition? Did they think she wanted to talk about her miserable ex? She flushed and looked down at her hand, then cleared her throat. "I—"

"Don't answer that, Mikaela," Thomas said. "It's none of our business."

"I just think it's odd she doesn't have a ring on her finger," Rob pressed.

Hopefully, her response would be the end of this line of questioning. "It's all right, Thomas." She looked at Rob. "The ring that was given to me was a family heirloom and had to be sized." Thank God that was the truth. Now she wouldn't have to go through the process of returning it. Had Joel bought her a brand new one, she'd be keeping it from the bastard, but since it'd been in his family for generations, she had no right to keep it.

Rob nodded and smirked at his dad, as

if to emphasize that the question had been logical.

Enough about her. "So, does anyone have a girlfriend?" Why did she look at Josh first? *You know why.*

She was met with a bunch of shaking heads and grunts before Thomas spoke up.

"They don't get out much. The land keeps us fairly busy."

Surely they could find the time for relationships, but she was pleased to know that Josh was not involved with anyone. When she set her empty wineglass on the table, Toby picked up the bottle and poured her another. She smiled at him and then looked back at Thomas. "What about you?"

"Me?" He chuckled. "Their mother died several years ago. I have no desire for another mate."

Mate? That was a bit primitive, but she laughed with him.

The rest of the evening went as smoothly as before the uncomfortable topic of Joel reared its ugly head, and not wanting to press her luck further, she excused herself as soon as the opportunity came.

She wanted a night of relaxation and

sleep after having such a hectic night last night. That bar had been seedy, but it was the only place open at that time of night, and she'd had to get away. Tonight, though, she wanted peace.

After she changed into her nightgown and opened her book, she heard the back door open and close like she'd heard the other nights. For some reason, all the guys went outside every night after dinner and had to have come back in late because she was always asleep before she heard them return. She had no idea what they did out there. She figured it wasn't work related since they all showered and changed before dinner and none of them mentioned a nightly duty on her tour today.

Okay, so she was tired, but she was also curious.

Curiosity won.

Enjoying her lingering liquid courage, she got out of bed, threw on a pair of jeans, and headed downstairs. She found a flashlight in the kitchen and walked out back to investigate. There were five sets of clothes piled along the deck. Did they all change into something else? If so, why did they leave their other clothes out here? Maybe they were in a hot tub. She felt a chill race down her spine at the thought of Josh sitting naked in a hot tub.

She looked around and didn't hear or see anything of the sort, so she headed into the woods.

———

JOSH LEFT the others and ran by himself because he just couldn't keep hearing the same lecture from his father or the same echoes of desires from his brothers. They were not going through the same thing he was. His feelings, needs, went way beyond the need to just bed her. He felt like he was doing a good job maintaining his control, but he felt his control slipping. He wanted her...badly. But all he could do right now was run like the devil himself was chasing him. Running helped clear his mind, and he'd take any relief he could get. He was in the middle of his downhill sprint when he caught a scent that stopped him cold.

Mikaela.

What was she doing outside? Her scent was strong, so it was easy to track. Once he found her, he stilled. She was near one of the cabins, but he couldn't shift and walk up to her. He needed to go get his clothes first if he was going to do that, but he didn't want to leave her now that he knew she was out here alone. He was going to anyway; he'd just have to hurry. He raced to the deck, clamped his teeth around his clothes, and raced to the trees beside the cabin. He changed quickly and walked toward her. She was peeking inside a window when he came up to her.

"Isn't that against the law?" Josh murmured right behind her.

She jumped around, her hand flying to her chest to cover her heart. "You scared the shit out of me!" she yelled with a giggle.

He laughed. "What are you doing out here, besides snooping around?"

"Nothing. Just snooping. But I'm glad you're here. I thought I saw a really big cat out there a few minutes ago."

He was sure she had. "Oh, I think our little tour scared you." He chuckled. When she smiled at him, he lost track of that thought. God, she had such a beautiful smile. He wanted to touch her, so he forced himself not to.

"Would you like to have a look inside?" He stepped toward the door.

"I already tried it. It's locked."

He smiled at her as he reached above the door and pulled a key off the jamb. Then he unlocked the door and stepped aside so she could walk in. When she passed by him, her body heat crashed over him like a tidal wave. It ignited his deepest longings for her, and he had no idea how he was going to rein it in. He was realizing too quickly that he just didn't want to anymore.

"I take it this is a guest cabin?" She looked around, noticing the sitting area to one side and a big bed to the other. Josh watched as her cheeks flushed when she took in the sight of the bed, and the last thread of his control snapped.

"Yes," he mumbled as he kicked the door shut behind him in one move and was on her in the next.

"Josh," she breathed.

"I-I tried. I just can't anymore." He slid his hands in that fiery red hair, and his lips nudged against hers, repeatedly, frantically. His hands fisted in her tresses as he panted into her mouth, their breaths becoming the only air for the other. God, he wanted to kiss her. He couldn't wait another second. He'd coaxed her lips apart, sliding his tongue home. The sensation was indescribable. He pulled one hand out of her hair to pull her body against him, and he crushed his lips to hers, hard, groaning in her mouth. She tasted of wine and woman. His woman.

Josh could kiss her forever, but he wanted more. He pulled away, scrambling with the buttons on her shirt, her whimpers fueling him further. He had to have her. There was no other choice for either of them anymore. She was his, and he was hers.

He kissed her neck as he unhooked her bra. When it fell to the floor, he stared at her breasts, and his frantic movements paused. He gently raked his fingers over her nipples, almost reverently, and groaned when they hardened for him. He swooped down and drew one rigid nipple into his mouth, flicking it with his tongue and then sucking it hard. He gave the other one the same attention while his hands worked to unfasten her jeans.

She tangled her hands in his hair and pulled his face back to hers, her eagerness almost his undoing. He shoved his tongue in her mouth while she unbuttoned his shirt. Before she was finished, he slid his hand into her jeans, slipping inside her cotton panties. When his finger grazed her clit, she pulled away gasping.

"Oh, God. You feel so good," she breathed.

Josh groaned, pulled his hand free, and picked her up. He carried her to the bed and removed the rest of their clothes. Once she was completely naked, he paused again, staring in awe.

"You're so beautiful, kitten." He bent over and kissed and licked his way down her belly to the apex of her thighs. He nudged her knees apart and settled between her legs as he continued to kiss and lick her hips and legs. When she began to squirm, he grabbed her thighs and dipped his head to lick her clit.

She cried out at the sudden spike in her pleasure, and he groaned at how wonderful she tasted. Much more potent than the lingering essence on his fingers that first night. He licked and sucked her labia, then plunged his tongue inside her, lapping up her cream as she fed it to him. She rocked her hips, trying to get him to focus on her clit, so his hands bracketed her hips and held her in place while he continued to fuck her with his tongue.

"Josh, oh, God. I-I can't take it anymore." She struggled to move her hips while he strained not to move his. His cock was rock hard and aching to be inside her. If he moved too much, he'd come right now.

"Mikaela, you taste so good, kitten. I want you to come on my fingers like you wanted to before." He moved one hand down, plunging two fingers inside her pussy while he moved his tongue closer to her clit. He felt her stiffen in anticipation, but he just circled it a few times, teasing her as long as she could stand it, testing his own endurance.

Her hands knotted in his hair and she tried to inch closer to him. "Please," she choked out.

He moaned, grinding his own hips in response to her plea. He couldn't take it anymore. His tongue rubbed her clit fiercely before sucking it into his mouth. Her back arched, and she went off like a bomb, screaming his name. God, she felt so good. He removed his fingers from her still pulsing pussy to swallow her cream, but he couldn't do this anymore. He had to have her completely.

Right now.

While Mikaela was enjoying the lingering sensations of her orgasm, Josh rummaged in the nightstand for a condom. His hands were trembling so much with anticipation that he could barely open the packet. When he grabbed his cock, he was so sensitive he had to fight the urge to stroke it. He strained to sheath his cock and glanced at Mikaela. She was breathtaking, but she also had her eyes opened wide with probably shock. Josh knew he had a big dick. He figured she was trying to gauge whether or not she'd be able to take him. He wasn't worried though.

Sliding over her, he covered her body with his and kissed her, passing the taste of her essence from his mouth to hers. She moaned softly as she licked and sucked at his lips, so he knew she liked tasting herself on him. He reached down and grabbed his cock, rubbing the head against her opening. He nudged just that bulbous head inside, then lifted her hips, coaxing her to wrap her legs around his waist. Once she did, he braced his hands beside her to support his weight, dug his head in the crook of her neck, and rolled his hips. Damn, but she was tight! Maybe he should've been worried. He entered her in increments, but he still strained to remain in control. He knew he couldn't plunge into her, but God, how he wanted to! When she stiffened underneath him and made a desperate whimpering sound, Josh knew she felt impossibly stretched and full, but he still had a few inches to go. Having a big dick wasn't what it was cracked up to be, but with some patience and coaxing, he'd get it in.

"Sorry," Josh breathed into her ear. "I know I'm kinda big." He stopped moving and kissed Mikaela's ear and neck, sliding one hand down between her legs. He braced his fingers on the top of her thigh and rubbed her clit with the pad of his thumb. She moaned and wrapped her fingers around his biceps, but didn't move her hips. He leaned his forehead against the side of her head and groaned, struggling not to thrust into that sweet haven. After a few moments of fingering her clit, she began to move her hips slightly, but he couldn't meet her thrusts; he knew she wasn't ready, but that didn't make it any easier on him to resist. In fact, he felt his control slipping rapidly. "Oh, God, Mikaela." He moved his thumb faster over her clit while his head rocked back and forth in her hair to distract himself from the sweet, tight fit of her pussy.

"Ahhh, you're going to make me come again."

"*Yes, kitten. Come for me.*" *Please, for the love of God, come now!*

She screamed when her climax hit, and he groaned when her pussy convulsed around his cock. "You feel so fucking good, kitten." He thrust inside her, hoping she was enjoying her orgasm too much to notice any pain he was causing her. He buried himself to the hilt and paused while she clung to him. She was still panting as she adjusted to his size. After a few moments, he traced her lips with his tongue, panting into her mouth, and started shallow thrusts to gauge her body's willingness. When she moaned and arched into his movements, he knew she was ready.

He fucked her with long, slow, full strokes, but she grabbed his ass and forced him in deeper. He couldn't resist her. He had to give her what she wanted. He picked up his pace, plunging harder and faster into her. He couldn't believe how quickly she adjusted to him once he was inside her. She felt too good. Perfect. So perfect that he barely maintained any constraint.

She clawed at his back as he plowed into her, and another orgasm detonated. He rode her through it, enjoying the feel of her pussy squeezing him, but trying not to get lost in that sensation. As soon as that happened, he knew he'd blow. She came again, digging her fingernails into his back. He only held on by a thread, which in and of itself was nothing short of miraculous at this point. He wanted to take her, mark her, make her his, but he knew he couldn't. He could only enjoy her like he'd enjoyed other women. He grabbed her hips and pounded in and out like a piston, crushing that depressing thought with brutal thrusts. She was not just some woman! He fucked her hard, losing his hold on the animal within.

When she came again, he couldn't hold out. He surged deep inside her and froze, throwing his head back with a roar that he knew didn't sound quite human, but was too absorbed to even care. He bent his head back into the crook of her neck, gulping in air as his chest heaved and, with a few short jabs of his cock, finished spilling his seed into the condom. With the last of his diminishing thrusts, his fangs slid out, the animal demanding he claim its mate. He turned his teeth away with great effort from the temptation her throat presented.

As he rested atop her, Josh's mind was spinning. Never, not once, had he ever lost control like that during sex. He'd always maintained control over his feral side, but he'd fucked her like a madman, and his fangs popped out, demanding he claim her. He felt he was in control now, but thinking of his brother, Eric, he figured he shouldn't chance it. He forced his fangs to retract, so he could turn his face back toward her neck. He kissed her shoulder and worked his way up to her lips.

"That was amazing," he breathed against her mouth before kissing her there.

"Mmm-hmm."

He pulled his face back to stare at her. Her tousled, red hair was beautifully chaotic, her blue eyes the softest of sky colors, and her chest, neck, and face sported a luscious flush of arousal. She was a goddess. "You're so beautiful."

She smiled at him and ran her fingers down his cheek. He leaned into her touch, suppressing the urge to purr at her caress. "We should probably head back."

Thank God she said it first because that was the next thing he was going to say. At least now he didn't have to look like some jerk who wanted to fuck her and leave her. He'd love nothing more than to stay. The thought of leaving was making some unnamed emotion squeeze at his chest, but right now, she was way too much of a temptation to his feral side for him to stay around her. He knew making love to her would awaken all his desires, but right now he couldn't seem to care enough to worry about all the repercussions. "Yeah, the others will be looking for me."

They got up, got dressed, and he escorted her out of the cabin and back to the main house. He rubbed soothing circles on the back of her hand as he held it, lost in his thoughts, trying to identify this crushing emotion that consumed him. He'd never felt anything like it before.

And now that he wasn't balls deep in her, he could think more clearly about what he should do. He hated the idea of avoiding her again. Even just thinking of doing that to her now made his animal roar inside. He couldn't do that, but he had to figure something out before talking to his father because he knew his dad would want to send her away. Whether she left early or not, Josh had to face the fact that Mikaela would be leaving. She had a life away from here. That crushing, all consuming emotion was back with a vengeance.

He walked her to her door, kissing her softly, longingly before escaping to his own room, the realization of his feelings almost crippling him.

How in the world was he going to let her go when he was in love with her?

CHAPTER EIGHT

MIKAELA GOT UP EARLY to have breakfast with the guys, so she could see Josh again right away. Last night had been the most powerful lovemaking she'd ever experienced. When Josh touched her, she melted into him, but what was even more wonderful was that he had the same reaction when she touched him. She wasn't the only one feeling a connection and acting on desire, and that thought thrilled her. As soon as she got up, she realized she couldn't wait for breakfast.

She brushed her teeth, threw on her robe, and made her way to the third door on the left.

Josh didn't answer her soft knocks, so she eased open the door. He wasn't in bed, but she noticed a light coming from underneath a door on the other side of the room. The last time she was in here, she hadn't paid much attention to the details, but she figured that door led to his bathroom. She closed and locked the bedroom door and tiptoed to the other door. *Yes!* She heard the shower running, so she could just slip in and join him. She took off her robe and nightgown, letting them fall to the floor, and gently opened the bathroom door. The room was filled with steam, so she couldn't see Josh.

But she could hear him.

The soft sounds of flesh on flesh, water squirting, and his low grunts told her that he was in there jerking off. Perfect.

Luckily, the showers here were custom without doors, so she was able to step in behind him without making a sound. He had a hand braced on the back wall while he worked his cock in his other hand. Not wanting to freak him out, she figured she shouldn't go right for his balls per his previous invitation. Instead, she rested her hands on his hips and kissed his back.

Josh froze.

Mikaela slid one hand up his chest and

the other down his belly to his groin and cupped his balls. She squeezed and tugged on his sac.

Groaning, he slowly started moving his hand again. After a few strokes, Mikaela wanted more from him. No, he wasn't going to be spilling his seed on the shower floor.

She maneuvered around him and dropped to her knees, running her tongue the length of his cock before he realized what was happening.

He gasped, let go of his cock, and adjusted the showerhead so that she didn't get pelted with water. When she kissed his engorged glans, his hands shot into her hair, and he bit off another groan. She licked the precome with relish, and his cock jerked in response. When she closed her lips around the head, his hands fisted tighter in her hair, and he groaned louder. She took him deep into her mouth, the head nudging the back of her throat.

"Oh, God, kitten. I was already close before..." He groaned again, his hips rocking as he took over control. He held her head firmly while he fucked her mouth. She grabbed the base of his shaft to control his thrusts, hollowing her cheeks as she sucked him. She couldn't take all of him, but she strained to take as much as she could, keeping one hand on his sac to fondle his balls. He moaned and fucked her mouth faster. She felt his balls draw up and knew he was about to go over, so she squeezed his sac and sucked in hard. He roared his release, pumping, pumping, pumping into her mouth, filling it with his come, and she swallowed everything he gave her. She kept sucking, licking, and swallowing until he was completely flaccid and bending over her head.

She released him slowly, and he helped her stand, embracing her once she was upright to support the both of them.

"Good morning," she mumbled into his chest.

He chuckled. "Yes, it is."

"I figured your offer to play with your balls was still open, so I took you up on it. I hope you didn't mind."

"Uh-uh. You can play with my balls anytime." He laughed. "You were already touching me in my fantasy, anyway. That's why you surprised me. Your scent was on my mind."

My scent? "I'm not wearing any perfume."

"Mmmm...I know." He nuzzled her hair.

She smiled and pulled away, stepping out of the shower. Now that she'd gotten what she'd come for, she needed to get ready for breakfast.

He grabbed her wrist. "Where are you going?"

"I'll shower after exercising, and I need to get ready for breakfast."

"But that's not fair." He leaned out of the shower. "I didn't get to pleasure you." The look in his eyes was a promise they'd both enjoy the pleasure he alluded to.

She wrapped a towel around herself and kissed him. "You pleasured me many, many times last night. It's the least I could do. Besides, you were going to come with or without me anyway."

"True." He smirked, but there was a glint in his green eyes. Before she could register the meaning of his gaze, he grabbed her arm and hauled her into the shower, towel and all. "But since you're here..."

He yanked the towel off her while his lips found hers. His tongue probed for entry, and she opened up for him, loving the feel of his tongue in her mouth. He kissed her deeply, his hands sliding down her ribs, gripping her thighs to wrap her legs around his hips. He shoved her against the wall of the shower and rubbed his growing cock against her slick sex. They both groaned at the contact.

"I'm going to fuck you, kitten," Josh growled. "Do you think you can take me?"

Whether or not she could, Mikaela was sure as hell going to try. No doubt about it! "Oh, yes, Josh. I want you to fuck me."

He slid his cock to her opening and pushed inside. She wrapped her arms around his neck and lifted up a little to let gravity help his invasion. She was a little sore from last night, but that only heightened the sensation for her. It didn't take long before he was fully seated inside her, and they both sighed with the small victory.

"God, kitten, what are you doing to me?"

His plea was so raw that Mikaela felt her throat tighten. Even though she was unable to speak, Josh didn't wait for a response. He started plunging into her.

She held on tightly, listening to their

shallow breaths and heated grunts, feeling his complete and total possession of her. He squeezed her ass as he mercilessly thrust into her, pinning her to the wall. Even at the height of passion, she was able to discern that his earlier comment could be construed as a sign of emotional weakness, but his actions now were nothing short of domination.

She gasped as her orgasm suddenly rocked her. He jostled her weight to one hand and lifted the other to grab her hair. His mouth closed over hers to capture her sounds of ecstasy, but then she was the one stifling his moan as he came. While he was still moaning with his climax, he pulled his hand out of her hair and ripped his mouth off hers, turning his face away. He pounded his fist against the tile and dug his head into his shoulder, whimpering.

Mikaela turned to face Josh and nuzzled the back of his head, wondering why he was looking away from her.

"Josh?" she whispered.

He shook his head, but after several seconds, he looked up and slowly eased her down. He cleared his throat as he finally faced her and started to smile, but he quickly dropped his forehead to hers before kissing her softly. He was hiding something from her, but she didn't understand what. She pulled away to ask him and saw blood running down his arm.

"What happened?" she asked, pulling his arm under the spray to rinse it off.

"I guess I bit down too hard to keep from crying out." He gave her a half smile as he pulled his arm free, but then sighed, looking distraught and closing his eyes while resting his forehead against hers again. "Mikaela, kitten, we didn't use any protection."

Ah, that explained it. Not a very responsible way to act, but at least it wasn't as bad as he'd feared. She took a deep breath. "Not that I'm condoning that, but I am on birth control. And, er, I'm clean."

"That's good. Me, too, on the latter." He smiled briefly, but still kept his eyes closed. She figured he'd be relieved, but he really didn't seem mollified at all.

Why was that?

———

JOSH KNEW he needed to tell Mikaela

something and fast. He didn't have to worry about birth control or diseases. He could only reproduce with a mate, and his kind seemed impervious to any illness that affected reproduction.

But coming inside her would leave a scent far stronger than if he were in his feline form and rubbed his scent glands all over her. His brothers, his *father*, would know as soon as they smelled her that he'd marked her with his scent. Even worse, his feline would sense it too. He already had enough control issues with fighting his feral self. When he was making love to her, he had to look away from her again to keep from sinking his fangs into her throat and taking her. He wanted to so badly that he bit himself to keep from biting her. And now he'd have to contend with the added attraction of his scent mixed with hers. She already smelled exquisite before.

Now she'd be his own personal catnip.

And his family would know.

"Can you take the day off?" Josh asked her as he picked up the soap and started washing her.

"Yeah, I guess so. Why?"

"We have a cave at the south side of the

property I'd like to show you." And keep *you away from the family until I figure out what the hell I'm going to do.*

She smiled at him. "That sounds like fun. We can head out after breakfast."

"No. We need to wait until the sun comes up before we head out." He leaned down and kissed her gently, letting his lips linger on hers. "And, ummm, I was thinking I'd bring you breakfast in bed."

Her smile seemed an acceptance, so they rinsed off and got out of the shower.

"So you're not freaked out about the condom thing?" she asked timidly as they donned their robes.

Josh took a deep breath and gave her a genuine smile. "Am I that transparent?" he asked with a small chuckle.

She briefly smiled. "I just don't want you to be worried."

Josh pulled her into his arms, stroking her back. "I just want to do what's best for you, Mikaela, and losing control like that makes me feel like I let you down." Which was the truth. She just wouldn't fully understand the reasons.

"Well, we'll be more careful next time."

He growled playfully. "You keep

talking like that, kitten, and we won't make it to the cave."

After seeing her back to her room and telling her to snuggle back in bed, Josh went down to the dining room. His family was already eating when he walked in. Of course his dad gave him the third degree about dragging his ass this morning, but he just shrugged him off. He only had one opportunity to sell this, and he couldn't muck it up.

"I ran into Mikaela last night when I left," Josh said casually, sipping his coffee.

Thomas put his cup down. "What? When? When you were out running?"

"Yeah. I shifted before she saw me, and we talked. She misses her fiancé and said something about spending the day in town to do some shopping to make herself feel better." He sighed and looked down, hoping this shit he was trying to sell would be bought.

Thomas cleared his throat. "You knew she was taken, Josh."

"It doesn't make it any easier, Dad."

His brothers got up, and Thomas sighed, dropping his napkin and standing up, too. "C'mon. Working will take your mind off things."

Josh ran his hands through his hair and looked down. "I-I don't feel like it. I didn't get any sleep last night. I think I'm going to just go back to bed for a while. Do you think you can handle everything without me today?" he asked, not looking up.

"Josh, don't let this get to you. I—"

"Too late, Dad. But you're right... She's taken, and she's not going to be in the house today, so I'm going back to bed. I'll meet up with you tonight for the run." He pushed himself away from the table and headed for the door.

"Josh," Jack said, making as if to follow.

"Let him go," Thomas said. "We can handle it today."

Josh waited around the corner for them to leave, and then he snuck back into the dining room, made a plate, and grabbed some coffee. He made it back up to Mikaela's room without detection and hoped his dad and brothers believed the story he'd fed them.

When Josh walked in, he discovered she'd fallen back asleep. Looking at her with her naked shoulders exposed and hair strewn across the pillow stole the breath from his lungs. He set down the pilfered items and locked her door before shrugging out of his clothes. He crawled in bed behind her, snuggled up against her back, and wrapped his arm around her waist. She stirred but didn't wake, and Josh was relieved. He could purr at this contact without worry.

And he did until he fell asleep with her in his arms.

Josh awoke later that morning to soft kisses on his cheek, and he couldn't help but smile.

"Good morning, sleepyhead."

He tightened his arms around her. "Good morning, kitten. I love waking up with you."

"Umm, I can tell." Mikaela rubbed her hand down his chest and wrapped her fingers around his dick.

He turned into her with a chuckle that quickly turned into a groan when she tightened her fist around him. He slid his hand up her thigh, hooked her leg over his hip, and lightly traced his fingertips along her inner thigh to her wet heat at the apex of her legs. She moaned and bent her head back onto the pillow. He closed his mouth over the beating pulse in her neck and sucked while sinking two fingers into her pussy, making her cry out his name. She pumped him faster, and he murmured words of lust through panting breaths.

"I want you to come inside me," Mikaela breathed.

His guttural sound made her clutch him tighter. "Oh, fuck, we—I don't have any condoms on me." It amazed him that he was able to even say that.

She stopped stroking him, and he made a small sound of protest, stopping his own ministrations. "Don't stop! I'm so close," Mikaela pleaded.

Josh continued fingering her while he rubbed himself against her leg since she hadn't started stroking him again. "Ah, kitten, I want to feel your hands on me." She gasped and grabbed his arm, and he could feel her pussy squeezing around his fingers as she came.

She pushed his shoulders back and sat astride him, sucking her juices off his fingers. She started rocking against his cock. "Tell me how you want it, Josh. Say it."

He grabbed her hips to grind harder

against her. "Oh, kitten, you're going to make me come like this," he rasped.

"Is that what you want?" She grabbed his wrists and held them above his head. She eased up so that his cock barely made contact with her pussy. He knew he could pull his arms free, but he rather liked her taking charge. "Or do you want to come on my tits or in my mouth?"

"Fuck, Mikaela, I'm going to come just from you talking like that." He thrust upward to deepen the contact, but she moved up to prevent it. She leaned down and kissed his ear.

"Say it, Josh."

"Your mouth. Put me in your mou—" He gasped when she quickly moved and took all of him into the wet haven he wanted. "Yes. Yes!"

She sucked him hard, and he snapped up in the bed, pulling her hair up to watch. Her ass was hiked in the air, and he caressed it as he watched her suck him off. So damn beautiful.

It didn't take long. Within moments, he was biting down on his bottom lip to keep from crying out when he came down her throat.

Josh pulled her to him, stroking her hair for what seemed like forever. Then needing to remedy the condom situation, he left to scour the cabins, collecting all that he'd found before returning to the warmth of her bed, her arms.

They never made it to the cave. They spent the day in bed, talking, laughing, playing. Loving.

His feline self had never been so content, and he'd never been as united to the animal as he was in this moment. He felt whole, and it was all Mikaela's doing.

But by the end of the day, he still didn't know how he was going to explain everything to his father.

He was in love, and he'd never been happier or more scared in all his life.

<hr>

CHAPTER NINE

MIKAELA AWOKE with something that she hadn't had in quite some time. She didn't realize it'd been missing until it'd returned to grace her presence.

Her smile.

Not only could she not remember the last time she'd been this happy, but she couldn't remember the last time the reason for her happiness was because of a man. Being a strong, independent woman had altered her ideals, thinking she didn't need a man to make her happy, and she hadn't even realized that line of reasoning had taken root in her. It was probably because of Joel. Joel and every other asshole she'd wasted time on. But now the man she couldn't seem to stop thinking about made her smile even bigger.

Josh. She'd spent the entire day with him yesterday, and she loved every single minute of it. She'd never been that open with anyone, and it felt great, but whenever they'd talk about his family, he'd say he'd deal with them and then changed the subject. She didn't understand his reluctance to discuss them, and he never asked her about her relationship with Joel. Mikaela had every intention of telling Josh the truth, but honestly, yesterday was about the two of them. Josh didn't talk about his family, and Mikaela didn't talk about Joel. But she knew she had to do it and do it soon.

She showed up at breakfast promptly at six, but the guys were scrambling to grab breakfast in a hurry. Of course, her eyes immediately sought out Josh, and he shared a tender smile with her.

"What's up?" she asked to no one in particular as she walked to the table.

Thomas eyed her briefly before responding. "There's a front moving in. We need to get prepared." He was dressed in work clothes like the rest of the guys, so he was obviously going to be working outside.

"What kind of front?"

"Winter weather," Jack explained as he turned his cup up to gulp the last of his coffee.

"Well, if you need me to do anything, let me know. I'd be happy to do what I can."

"That's not necessary, Mikaela," Thomas said without making eye contact. She figured he was just worried about this weather moving in.

"Dad, she could contact the lumber companies and cancel the scheduled pickups this week," Rob suggested.

"Absolutely not. She is not my secretary. I can do it when I get back," he barked.

"Really, Thomas. I don't mind." She glanced at Josh, but he was watching Thomas.

There was a pause while Josh and Thomas stared at each other and then he cleared his throat. "All right. Come with me, and I'll show you who needs to be contacted." He turned to his sons. "Boys, get outside and get started without me. We have to move fast if this storm is as big as they're predicting."

By the time Thomas was finished giving her the contact information for the lumber companies, which didn't take long at all considering how agitated he was, the snow had started falling.

With the way Thomas was either eyeing Mikaela or avoiding eye contact altogether, she figured Josh had told him what happened. Well, maybe not everything, but enough to explain that they were becoming involved with one another. It seemed like Thomas wasn't very happy about this news, so she'd have to come clean about Joel with Thomas too. Hopefully everyone would understand, and hopefully, the weather wouldn't be as bad as they were saying. She didn't want to get stranded here if Thomas had an issue with her getting involved with his son.

Then again, she really liked the idea of being stranded here with Josh. That thought put a smile on her face as she started to work.

She spent the day thinking about him while doing the tasks given to her. She stayed on the phone, rescheduling pickups and dealing with other things that made absolutely no sense to her since she'd never dealt with lumber issues before. Most of the companies were understanding and even appreciative for the heads up to the incoming weather, but there were a few where she had to flex her legal muscle to get them to cooperate.

By that evening, the ground was covered in nearly two feet of snow with heavy snow still falling. The guys worked as much as they could, cleaning up previously cut trees and storing the small and large equipment. Most of that stuff was made to endure the elements, but when heavy snow was predicted, Thomas said they didn't take chances.

She knew the men spent most of the day outside in the harsh conditions, so they probably enjoyed the moment when they could come inside to shower before eating. Mikaela never got around to exercising today, but she needed a shower, too, so when they all came in, she used that as her opportunity to freshen up. When she reached the dining room, she could see that everyone was exhausted. The guys were all nursing their drinks, and there was a bottle of wine sitting at her place setting. Josh rose and walked over to open the bottle and pour her a glass.

"Thanks," she whispered, bringing the glass up to her lips.

"Oh, you can thank me later," he murmured.

"I intend to."

"Mmmm...I can't wait." He smiled.

The others crowded around the table while Jeffery brought out the food, and everyone took their seats.

"Thanks for your help today, Mikaela," Thomas said as he placed his napkin in his lap.

"It was my pleasure, Thomas."

"I hope it didn't set you back too much on your legal work."

"Oh, no, I'm already ahead of schedule." No need to tell him how ahead she was. She had no intention of leaving sooner than scheduled now that she was enjoying some hot, sweaty private time with Josh.

"That's good. You should contact your office and let them know about the storm, so they do not worry."

"I already did. I told them I'd check in once the weather clears."

Thomas nodded.

Everyone ate and chatted about the first big snowfall of the season. The guys were busy comparing it to other major events in the past, but Mikaela just spent her time watching Josh's mouth move when he spoke. A few times he caught her staring, and smiled and winked at her when no one else was looking. That innocent gesture made her feel like a teenager with her first crush, but as she thought about that, the reality of her feelings came crashing down. Josh wasn't just a crush. In the course of her stay, she'd fallen in love with him. How was that even possible? The thought made her feel so happy...and so confused.

The door opened, and Jeffery walked in carrying a cordless phone. "Ms. Patterson, there is an urgent call for you."

Her eyes widened, and she swallowed her food. "Oh?" She stood, taking the phone.

"Yes, ma'am. It's a Mr. Youngblood."

She crushed the phone to her chest to shield her voice. "*What?*" she whispered. "What did he say?"

Jeffery lowered his voice. "Nothing, ma'am. He just insisted on speaking to you right away."

Shit, shit, shit!

Mikaela nodded and slowly put the phone to her ear, stepping away from the table in a daze. "Hello?"

———

JOSH'S EYES locked onto Mikaela as soon as she answered the phone. Who the hell was Mr. Youngblood, and why was he calling her?

"I'm fine," she said curtly into the phone.

She didn't sound fine to Josh. She sounded pissed.

"It's a little too late for that, Joel."

Joel? Joel! CPA Joel? Fiancé Joel? Josh felt his hackles rise as if he were in cat form and a hiss slipped out his throat.

"Hmm, well, you can take your apology, roll it up into a nice little ball, and shove it up your ass!" She hung up the phone, sat back at the table, and took a drink of her wine.

Josh's heartbeat quickened, ringing in his ears. His hands shook as he stared intently at her, his mind unable to grasp what was happening. It was probably just a fight, he tried to tell himself. Couples fought all the time.

"Er, is everything all right, Mikaela?" Thomas asked awkwardly.

"Mmm-hmm." She picked up her fork and took a bite of her food.

His dad seemed to be scrambling for words while the other men were intently focused on her. "Um, was that your fiancé on the phone?" he asked timidly.

"He wishes," she mumbled into her glass as she took another swig.

"I beg your pardon?" Thomas asked slowly. "Was that or was that not your fiancé?"

She sighed and looked at him. "He was about a month or so ago." Mikaela watched Thomas's eyes get bigger by the second and the blood rush out of his face, right about the time five distinct forks dropped out of five different hands and crashed onto five separate plates. "What?"

Josh shut his eyes, the enormity of her confession too much to process. But he had to stay focused, so when he opened his eyes, he tried to watch everyone.

"You mean you are *not* taken?" Thomas barely whispered.

"Taken? What? What's that? What's wrong?" She glanced around the table incredulously.

"Engaged or at least involved with someone."

She immediately looked contrite. "I'm sorry. I meant to clear this up earlier. I *was* engaged to Joel until I found him... Well, until about a month or so ago. I wasn't ready to tell Bill, so he assumed I still was engaged."

Mikaela smiled at Josh, and he understood what she was trying to convey. She was trying to tell him she was free to be with him. But she didn't understand. Before he had a chance to even voice anything, he caught movement out of the corner of his eye.

Toby had leaned closer to her. He growled right next to Mikaela, and she gasped, scooting her chair back to get away from him.

"Don't!" Thomas yelled. But Josh didn't think Mikaela knew who his father was speaking to. Hell, *he* wasn't sure if his dad was talking to Toby or to Mikaela. He just watched her freeze while he prepared to act, shifting his eyes to Toby. He just didn't know what would happen. None of them had ever been in a situation like this before. Not and lived through it.

"What the fuck is wrong with you?" she barked at Toby.

The next three seconds went by faster than expected. She was sitting at a table with five angry-looking men one moment, and then the next, only his dad remained looking distraught.

Josh's brothers had shifted, so he shifted on instinct to protect Mikaela. Now she was staring at four huge mountain lions. This was so not how he wanted her to find out!

She opened her mouth to scream, but nothing came out. She was frozen. The cats didn't move, but Toby was right next to her, growling and sniffing her leg. She started to scoot her chair again.

"Mikaela! Don't move," Thomas ordered.

"What the hell is going on here?"

"Long story. Basically, we are all mountain lion shifters. Our feral side spends its life searching for a mate. Once we find her and take her as our mate, she also becomes a shifter. Our humanity respects mating bonds already in place, hence why I only allow taken women on the property. However, our feral side does not wait for a mating approval with an untaken woman. Out in the wild, males dominate the females and take what they want. My sons are all in their feral forms now."

"And they all want me?" she whispered.

"They all want a mate."

She glanced at the lion where Josh was sitting. But he couldn't look at her; he had to stay focused on protecting her from his brothers. His eyes shifted to each of the cats, but none of them looked at him. They all watched her.

"Josh?" she whispered.

At the sound of her beautiful voice, his eyes shot to her, but he looked away quickly. He couldn't risk it. He didn't want his brothers to hurt her, but if *he* were the one to hurt her, he'd never be able to forgive himself. *Dad, explain things to her.*

"Josh wants me to explain that he's the only one who has any control right now, but it's very slim. He's more worried about protecting you than claiming you. He doesn't want any of the others to hurt you."

"What do you mean he wanted you to tell me that? How do you know?"

"We can speak telepathically. The other night when you caught Rob laughing? It was because they were discussing things privately."

Toby growled louder, and Mikaela made as if to move.

"Please, Mikaela, don't run. You'll just excite them. They like the chase. I'll try to reason with them. Just give me time."

She nodded. "Josh, I—"

"Don't, Mikaela. He's trying to resist you. If you force him to focus on you, he'll be the one you'll need to worry about the most."

"W-why is that?"

"Because he's the *closest* one to you." *Because he's fucked you already*, he added silently for Josh's benefit.

At least he didn't voice it out loud, though Josh didn't give a shit what his dad really thought about his relationship with her.

Toby's fur stood up, and he hissed at her. Josh jumped on the table and growled at him. Toby growled back at Josh and flinched at Mikaela, trying to make her move so he could chase her.

She grabbed her stomach, and Josh could see that reality was sinking in for her. If he could just get her out of here and explain everything himself...

"Oh, God, I'm going to be raped by a big scary kitty cat," she muttered, looking around the room, "or by a bunch of them."

Like hell! Hearing her frightened voice ignited Josh's anger. He'd kill anybody who hurt her!

Get her out of here, Dad! Toby, I swear I'll rip your fucking throat out if you touch her!

I'm closer to her, Josh. If you interfere with my mating, I'll kill you, Toby growled.

I'm right behind you, Toby. I can get to her before you can, Rob taunted, inching closer.

Hell, I'm faster than all of you. If she runs, she's mine! Jack declared.

Josh jumped across the table and stared down at Toby. He flinched but didn't move. *This is your last warning, Toby. I can kill you from here. Now back off!*

As soon as you attack him, the others will use the opportunity to jump in,

Thomas warned. He didn't want to say it out loud, lest he'd scare Mikaela more than she already was. Josh was pleased his dad was at least trying to help her as much as he could, but Josh knew he'd have to fix this himself.

And he wasn't waiting another second.

He jumped off the table, plowing into Toby's side, making him stumble back. Now Josh shielded her from all his brothers. He growled loudly at them. *Mine!* He wasn't going to allow anyone to claim his mate. She belonged to him, damn it!

His side brushed against her leg as he staked his claim, and he instinctively purred from the contact, distracting himself. He turned toward her and purred louder, rubbing against her. Her hands were dangling down, so he licked her fingers, nudging them to pet him. Her touch was the most exquisite thing in his regular form, but in his feline form it was pure bliss.

"Don't, Mikaela. He could turn on you."

Josh's head whipped to his father, and his purring turned to growls. *I'm* not *going to hurt her!*

Then let me get her to the safety of her room, and each of you to the cabins.

Josh didn't want to leave her, but he knew he had to prove his strength to his father. He nodded.

"Mikaela, Josh is going to help me get you to your room. You can stay there until I get them outside. Normally, I'd have you leave right away, but we're all stranded here until the storm passes."

"Okay."

Thomas walked around the table, and he and Josh escorted her out of the dining room amidst growls and hisses of protest. Once they were out, Thomas locked the door and instructed Jeffery to guard it until he returned. Thomas practically dragged Mikaela to her room while Josh followed, staying a few steps behind to block her from an attack if his brothers got loose. Once Mikaela arrived at her room, she turned to look at Josh.

"Go inside, Mikaela," Thomas warned.

Josh was unable to stifle the low growl that bubbled up at his father's interference. He knew she wanted to talk to him, but now his dad wouldn't even allow that. Thomas shot him a look for his defiance, so

Josh just dropped his head and turned. Knowing that Mikaela was now safely in her room, his dad would put them all in the cabins outside.

And he'd do everything in his power to keep Josh from seeing her again.

CHAPTER TEN

Day after day, Mikaela stayed quarantined in her room like some diseased patient. Like *she* was the one with a problem. Right. She was stuck with a bunch of men who turned into big ol' cats. She'd think that they were the ones who needed quarantining. Men who turned into animals? How was that even possible? This wasn't some sci-fi crap. People did not turn into animals! So why did all these guys do that?

If she really thought about it, some things made sense, though. She'd heard Josh make noises that sounded animalistic on more than one occasion. They all went out at night and didn't come back until long after she was asleep. They were probably out hunting or running or using their trees as giant scratching posts. They lived out in the middle of nowhere and apparently never left the premises since Josh hadn't gone after her when she went to the bar the other night. She wondered why he didn't, but now it made sense.

She hated being stuck here, but as she looked out her window at the snow-covered ground, she realized she wasn't the only one stuck. The guys must be quarantined just like she was. Over the last few days, she hadn't seen any of them, nor had she heard anybody but Jeffery in the hall outside her door, which was only when he'd come to bring her meals. That meant they were not staying in their rooms. She just didn't understand everything.

But she wanted to.

Against her better judgment, she wanted to talk to Josh. She longed to be in his arms and hear what he had to say about all this. She knew he had to be worried how she was taking the news that he turned into a cat, and honestly, it freaked her the hell out! But after the first day or two, she started to think more about the man and less about the animal. She knew they were one and the same, but she couldn't let herself focus solely on his animal side. He was a man, too.

A man she loved.

And now Thomas was keeping Josh from her. She knew how she felt about him, but she didn't know how he felt about her. When they were alone, everything seemed wonderful. But Thomas said their feral sides wanted a mate. Did Josh only see her as a potential mate for his kitty cat side? If so, would any available—or "untaken," as Thomas had so eloquently put it—woman do? The thought that Josh didn't feel about her the way she felt about him made her stomach churn. Unrequited love sucked; there was no other feeling about it. If Josh just wanted her for his mountain lion within and didn't care about feelings at all, she didn't know how to accept that. If Josh mated with her just because she was an available woman, she'd be stuck with him forever. Stuck with a man she loved who didn't love her back. That would be unbearable.

If she could just talk to Josh and get some answers, she'd feel better. And the more she thought about that, the more she wanted to do something about it. She was a grown-ass woman for crying out loud! And a lawyer who understood her rights about unlawful imprisonment. Okay, so she was stretching it, but she really didn't care. If she didn't get out of here, she'd go crazy.

After devising an escape plan, she picked up the phone on the nightstand and called Jeffery to initiate it, telling him some story about needing a snack. Then she went into the bathroom and twisted the faucet so that water trickled out, and she put the vanity chair right outside the bathroom door. When Jeffery knocked, she let him in, and he put her food on the table by the door.

"Hey, Jeffery, can you look at the sink? I can't get the water to turn off. It's bad enough being stuck in here, but a dripping faucet is maddening."

"Yes, ma'am."

He walked into the bathroom, and Mikaela pulled the door closed, wedging the vanity chair underneath the doorknob to keep it shut.

Jeffery pounded on the door, but she didn't stick around to hear his pleas. She quickly ran out of the room, locking the door and taking the key that Jeffery left in the knob. She covertly traipsed down the hall, keeping her eyes on her immediate surroundings, looking for any sign of Thomas.

Or the others.

As far as she knew, Thomas put them outside, but that could've meant anything. They were part animal. They could be out running around and living in the woods for all she knew, but she had to find Josh. As she ran down the stairs, she stumbled and caught herself on the railing, cursing below her breath. She rubbed her ankle, examined her foot, and looked up—right into the eyes of Thomas.

"Mikaela."

Well, ain't that about a bitch?
"Thomas."

"What are you doing out of your room?"

"Oh, well, see, I was going to step outside and get some fresh air." She shrugged her shoulders, feigning nonchalance.

"I can't let you do that." He stepped closer to her.

"Thomas, you can't keep me locked up."

"It's for your own safe—"

She sliced her hand in the air, cutting him off. "I'm free to leave if I choose. I understand we're snowed in, but I can walk out of here on my own two feet, leave your property, and can probably even hitchhike since the highway should be passable by now. Granted, it's not an ideal situation, but it's much better than being locked up!"

"Look, I'm sorry for all this, but I'm doing it to protect you. If you really want to chance leaving, let me, er, take an ATV to the main road and see if a lane has been cleared for travel."

"Thanks."

"But I want you to stay in your room until—"

"Thomas, I'm not going to stay cooped up like some caged animal."

"Interesting choice of words." He sighed, shaking his head. "I'll give you the key. Just lock the door from the inside."

She let him take her back up to her room, not mentioning the fact that she already had Jeffery's key. If Thomas had another one, she'd gladly take it, too. Keys were the least of her problems, though.

After Thomas sprang Jeffery from the bathroom, she was left to stew over her misguided attempt. Her little plan backfired. Ugh! She'd really screwed up. All she wanted was to talk to Josh, but all she managed to do was expedite her removal from the property.

And once she was gone, she knew she'd never be allowed back.

CHAPTER ELEVEN

Three days. Three damn days without seeing her. Josh couldn't stand it. He could not stand it! He proved to his father that he wasn't a threat to her, but Thomas still refused to allow him to see her. Once the others got away from her, they wanted to stay in the cabins; they didn't even shift at night to run and hunt. None of them wanted to take the chance of forcing a mating because they knew what that would mean.

Josh didn't care. He wanted to talk to her, make sure she was all right, explain what had happened. He was in love with her, and deep down, he knew she felt the same way about him. He was positive he could control his feral side with her. She was never taken. The whole time she was here. Just because she confirmed it verbally shouldn't matter.

And his father was standing between Josh and his future mate. He wouldn't force her into it, but he knew she'd be his. She already *was* his for all intents and purposes.

Josh walked into the main house and passed his father's opened door. He stood as soon as he saw Josh.

"Josh, do not—"

He kept walking. "I'm not going into her room. I just want to talk to her. I can do that through her door."

"I don't think that's wise."

"I don't give a damn what you think." He kept walking until he reached her door. "Leave us alone, please. It's bad enough I can't talk to her face-to-face. The last thing I need is an audience." Not waiting for a response from his dad, he knocked on her door. "Mikaela, it's Josh. I need to talk to you but don't open the door."

"O-okay."

Josh cocked his head to the side and stared at his father with his brow raised, waiting for him to leave. He nodded reluctantly and stepped away.

Josh leaned his head against the door, taking a deep breath. He could smell her luscious scent through the wood. God, how he missed her. "Kitten, I'm so sorry about what happened the other night. I know you had to have been really frightened. I need you to know that I'd never let anything happen to you."

"Why didn't you tell me?" She sounded like she was leaning against the other side of the door. She was so close, but still out of reach.

"We're sworn to secrecy. It's too dangerous for us if anyone finds out. Why didn't you tell me you weren't engaged?"

"I figured you'd figure it out when I slept with you."

He laughed softly, tracing circles on the wooden door. "No, I didn't."

"I miss you," she barely whispered.

"Oh, God, kitten, I miss you too. I don't know how it happened, but I-I... *Shit*. I hate saying this through the door." He wanted to tell her that he loved her, but he wanted to see her face, touch her skin. He heard her fumbling with the doorknob, and the door swung open. He stared at her, unshed tears glistening in her eyes.

"Tell me what?" she breathed.

He stepped through the door, shut it, and locked it. "You're not afraid of me?"

"No," she whispered, stepping closer to him.

He stiffened and shut his eyes at her nearness. "Ahh, kitten, I'm not sure if I can do this," he whispered. He wanted to take her right now, his feline fighting for control.

"What did you want to tell me?" she pressed, walking forward, ignoring his concern.

He cleared his throat and opened his eyes. "That I love you."

Her breath caught, and her tears leaked over. "I love you too, Josh."

At her admission, his control snapped.

MIKAELA TOOK another step toward him, reaching out for him, but hesitated when she saw his eyes glaze over. A feral sound crawled up his throat. "You're mine," he growled.

Uh-oh.

"Josh?"

There were no words. He took her in

his arms and kissed her, hard. He moaned as he clung to her, forcing her body against his. She understood that his feral side was taking over, so she couldn't fight him off even if she wanted to.

She didn't want to.

She tangled her hands in his soft brown hair and pulled herself up, wrapping her legs around him, rubbing her body against his hard dick like a cat in heat. He walked her over to the bed, falling on top of her. Even though she understood what was happening, she couldn't just give up complete control. Not yet. Deep down, she realized he'd have to prove himself to her. Prove that he was alpha enough, worthy enough to take her, make her his. Mikaela didn't think about all the consequences of what that meant for her; she just wanted Josh forever.

They both kissed and nipped at each other's lips, fighting for control. He yanked her shirt up and slipped his fingers under her bra. He plucked at her nipples, which turned into stiff buds immediately under the delicate lace. She grabbed his shirt and started pulling it up, and he broke away from the kiss to divest himself of it in one fluid motion. Within two seconds, he crushed his mouth back to hers, shoving his tongue into her mouth. He ripped her shirt open, buttons flying everywhere. He sat up on his knees, pulling her with him, and tried to pull her shirt all the way off, but she was busy fumbling with the button on his jeans, which blocked his progress.

"Take off your shirt. Now." He growled in her ear, and she immediately complied. God, he sounded so sexy. It took every ounce of willpower not to give in to him totally.

Once her shirt was off, he unhooked her bra and flung it to the side. He pushed her back down on the bed and bit her nipple, making her cry out. Then he laved it to ease the pain before sucking it to the roof of his mouth. While he sucked one nipple, he pinched and pulled on the other, and there was nothing gentle about his touch. He was showing her that he was the dominant one.

But she wasn't relinquishing her dominance just yet. She managed to flip him on the bed when he was distracted with her tits so that she was now on top. He growled in protestation, but didn't right her. He was too immersed in her breasts. He continued sucking her nipples until she slid her hand into his pants and stroked his cock through his boxers.

He released the tight suction on her nipple with a wet popping sound and grabbed the sides of her jeans. He pushed her off him and yanked her pants and panties down in one motion, then tossed her back onto the bed and pulled her clothes completely off in another.

Not being outdone, she sat up and reached for his pants, but he tried to push her back to the bed. She refused to give up.

"Take your pants off, Josh."

He growled, but he stopped pushing on her, stood up, and pulled his pants off. He stared at her briefly while she scooted farther on the bed. She lifted her hand and crooked a finger in invitation for him to join her. He growled again and crouched down, slowly crawling on the bed toward her like a predator stalking its prey. Slight unease crept into her, but she shook it off. It was only because this was new territory for them both.

"Tell me what you want, Josh," she said while she played with her nipples.

He growled louder, still advancing.

"Uh-uh. I want to hear you say it."

"I want to fuck you and bite you. Make you mine." His voice was a gravelly interpretation of his regular speech.

"Is that how you claim a mate?" she asked, trailing her hand down her belly to her pussy.

He watched her hand. "Yes. You must submit yourself to me." His head popped to stare into her eyes. "You *will* submit."

"Maybe later. Not right now." She smiled coyly at him.

He growled angrily at her, grabbed her ankles, and yanked her closer to him. He started to climb on top of her, seeming as if his feral side didn't want to engage in any more foreplay. He wanted to take her. Now.

She wasn't having it.

They grappled, rolling around on the bed, kissing, biting, licking, sucking, fighting for dominance. They were both panting with the effort it took to dominate the other. When she worked her way down his body, she wrapped her mouth around his cock and looked up at him. She knew she couldn't growl like he could, but she bared her teeth and tried anyway. His eyes grew big in alarm with her trapping him, but then he narrowed his eyes and leaned back. She figured he'd realized this was a fight worth losing for the moment.

She sucked his cocked all the way to the back of her mouth, forcing as much down her throat as she could. He groaned and fisted his hands in her already tousled hair, thrusting his hips up so she could take more. She squeezed his sac to the point of pain while she sucked him as hard and deep as she could. He groaned again, sounding more like a man in the heights of pleasure than an animal staking its claim. The more she sucked, the more pliant he became, moaning and rubbing his fingers in her hair, softening his grip.

"Oh, God, kitten, don't stop," he breathed.

She had no intentions of stopping anytime soon, but she pulled her mouth off and stroked him with her hand. "You want to come in my mouth? How very naughty of you, Josh."

He thrust his cocked between her fingers while he groaned. "Mikaela, I just want to come while you've got the upper hand. If I get control, I'm going to...oh, God, that feels so good...ugh, I'm going to bite you against your will. If I come...oh, yes, like that, kitten. Oh, my God, that feels so fucking good. Ahhhhhh, if I come, I can get away before I do something you don't want." He whimpered when she stroked him faster, and he rocked his hips in time with her hand.

She squeezed his sac and sucked him again. He groaned loudly, bucking his hips. "Yes, *yes*, I'm going to come, kitten. I want you to swallow all of it."

She felt his balls drawing up and knew her window of opportunity was upon her if she was going to take it.

She was. She'd come too far to turn back now.

Mikaela pulled his cock out of her mouth, dropped his balls, and backed away.

"W-what are you doing?" he asked breathlessly, propping himself on his elbows.

She got off the bed and stepped back. "I'm making a run for it."

His breath caught. "No, Mikaela, I-I'll chase you." He shook his head, shut his eyes, and wrapped his hand around his cock. She guessed he was just going to finish himself off to protect her. She couldn't let that happened. She'd just have to provoke him.

"Let go of *my* cock, Josh. You don't touch yourself unless I give you permission."

His eyes flashed to hers, and she saw them glaze over again. He dropped his cock, a low growl escaping him.

"That's right. You do what you're told because I'm the only alpha in this room."

His growl grew more pronounced. Any other time, she'd realize it was crazy to provoke a man struggling with domination, but she knew that was exactly what she needed to do. She backed away, taunting him, making him come after her. Josh flipped, landing on his hands and knees, crawling across the bed and jumping off. She turned as if to run to the door, and he caught her by the waist and threw her up against the door, her legs instinctively wrapping around his hips.

"Damn it, Mikaela! Do you know what you're asking? If not, you're really underestimating my control."

Oh, she knew what she was asking. She wanted to be his. She was never surer of anything else. "Take me, Josh."

His face immediately transformed to that of a powerful, determined being. He hadn't turned into a mountain lion, but he didn't look very human, either. He growled, putting her on the floor and maneuvering her on her hands and knees. He hovered over her, his chest pressed against the length of her back, roughly licking and kissing her shoulder. "I'm going to bite you right here after I fuck you." He sat up, grabbed her shoulders, and shoved her to the floor, leaving only her ass hiked up in the air, in a position of total submission. Without warning, he took her with one deep thrust.

"Josh!"

He pulled out slowly and slammed into her again. And again. And again. Keeping her teetering on the border of pleasure and pain, he started out slowly, but his feral side wanted to take his mate quickly, so he did. He fucked her hard and fast, her cries of passion fueling his own. She came suddenly, and he howled when her pussy fisted around his cock. But that didn't slow him down. He plowed into her again and again until she screamed his name over and over with one climax after another. When she was sobbing for breath, her will completely gone, his dominance proven, he pulled out smoothly, turned her around, and sat her astride him. He guided her gently back onto his cock, and she rode him slowly while he kissed and caressed her, touching her tenderly, lovingly.

"I love you, Mikaela," he murmured.

"I love you too."

They both panted and clung to each other, the dynamic of their coupling totally altered. When her next climax hit, he went with her. Throwing his head back with a roar of completion as he pumped his seed inside her, his fangs slid out, but this time, he didn't hide them from her.

She reached up and stroked his teeth, his lips curling with a snarl at her intimate touch. Josh may have been sated, but his beast obviously wasn't.

"Take me," she whispered.

He yanked her hand off his teeth and bit into her shoulder just above her collarbone without warning.

She cried out as she dug her fingers into his soft hair. The pain quickly turned into euphoria as her body hummed and pussy fisted on his softening cock. When he pulled his teeth out, he laved the bite while a rumble built in his chest—a purr. She stroked his hair, and he purred louder.

They held each other like that, unmoving, for what seemed like an eternity, neither one wanting to let the other go.

"So what happens now?" Mikaela asked.

Josh kissed his mark of possession and traced his lips up the side of her neck to her mouth. He kissed her on her lips before responding.

"I'm not really sure," he mumbled against her lips. "The last time any of us tried this was when Eric took a mate."

She gasped. "Your deceased brother?"

"Yeah, he forced a mating with his friend's ex-wife. He didn't know they were divorced until after she came here to visit him. It didn't end well. But *I* didn't force this mating." He chuckled. "You submitted willingly."

"Mmmmm... Yes, I did."

"So I imagine we'll compare our experience with that of what we know of Eric's and try to help my brothers." He slowly pulled his cock out of her, and they both groaned with the drag of flesh against flesh.

"In the meantime, you need to shift, kitten." He stood and opened the door.

"Oh, right!" She smiled and was going to ask how, but she realized she knew. Within seconds, she was a beautiful mountain lion standing next to Josh who'd also shifted.

Her mate.

She was no longer untaken.

I'll always belong to Josh, she thought.

I like the sound of that, kitten.

She purred at hearing his voice in her mind, feeling his love wash over her.

She never would've guessed she'd fall in love so quickly, but it was impossible to avoid when she was surrounded by woods —Josh Woods.

And now she'd get to spend the rest of her life with the one she loved.

Cabo had nothing on this.

EPILOGUE

JOSH PANTED as he and Mikaela lay sprawled across their bed, their naked bodies tied together in a sweaty heap of arms and legs. God, he'd never get used to making love to his wife.

"Damn, kitten." He nuzzled her hair as she was draped across his chest, eliciting a purr out of her. She'd taken to this new life better than he could've hoped for. She'd not only embraced him as her mate, with so much love and trust it humbled him, but she'd also connected to his family as if she'd always been a part of their lives. Josh was grateful every day for the love they'd found, and he knew how rare it was for someone like him. How dangerous—considering he came from a family of mountain lion shifters whose instinct to mate with any available woman had deadly fucking consequences. Yeah, he was the luckiest man alive for many reasons, not to mention his little kitten was a hellcat in the sack. "Next time, I get to tie *you* up."

"Mmm, I think that can be arranged."

He chuckled when she used her teeth to tug the bindings loose at his wrists. Once he was freed, he pulled her to him, kissed her neck, and caressed her arms.

"I've been thinking," she said.

Uh-oh. He loved her dearly, but that didn't sound good. "Yes?" he prompted, giving her one last kiss before pulling away to stare into her beautiful blue eyes.

"You know how we've talked about finding a way to help your brothers with the whole mating issue?" She waved her hand like she was downplaying the "issue," as she'd called it, and Josh knew instantly his little kitten was exercising her legal muscle to craft her words accordingly. He hid his smile. She should really know better than to try to draw him in like that. But he guessed it was too ingrained in her to shut that off.

"Of course. I take it you have an idea."

Her face lit up like the brightest star in the sky on the clearest of nights. So, why did he get a sinking feeling?

"Yes. Now I don't think you'll like this, but I think it's worth a shot. I mean, we have to do *something*. I think we have a duty to help your brothers find potential mates. We're mated, so we know it's possible. But we can't just decide their fates, you know? It's not like we can bring a bunch of unmated women out here and let them have it. It'd be mass hysteria with a little too much killing and not enough loving. We need to be practical about it. We need to make sure—"

"Mikaela, kitten, spit it out." So she did.

And she was right.

He didn't like it.

WHEN KRISTA'S colleague asks for her help on the Woods estate, she's eager to assist, but she gets the feeling Mikaela has an ulterior motive. Not that it matters. Krista might be a dang good attorney, but she's horrible with men. Why else would she still be a virgin? Find out just how feral Toby gets around her in ***Surrounded by Pleasure***, the second book in the Woods Family Series.

LIKE YOUR HOT alpha men with a side of danger? The Bang Shift Series contains full-length, contemporary romantic suspense novels, featuring mercenaries, mechanics, and the mafia! Start this hot, wild ride with ***Brody***, the first book in the Bang Shift Series. FREE on all retailers!

HEY, y'all!

Thank you for reading my book. :) If you enjoyed it, I'd be very grateful for a review. If you didn't like it, then share that, too... as long as your review is honest, that's all that matters.

And ice cream. Ice cream matters, too.

Xoxo,

Mandy

Surrounded by Temptation

Surrounded by Secrets

Young Adult written as M.W. Muse

Goddess Legacy

Goddess Secret

Goddess Sacrifice

Goddess Revenge

Goddess Bared

Goddess Bound

 Mandy Harbin is a *USA Today* Bestselling author who loves creating stories that explore the complexities of everyday relationships...with some kissing thrown in. She is a Superstar Award recipient, Reader's Crown and Passionate Plume finalist, and has achieved Night Owl Reviews Top Pick distinction many times. She also writes young adult romance as M.W. Muse because teens like kissing, too.

After graduating college and working many years in technology, she threw caution to the wind and began studying writing at the UALR. Years of trashed manuscripts and rejections eventually led to contracts and representation. With over thirty books published, she now serves on the board of her local writing chapter.

Mandy lives in a small, Arkansas town with her husband and their bossy dog, enjoying her own happily ever after...with some kissing thrown in.

www.mandyharbin.com